Juliet Joins
the Guides

Juliet frowned. 'They're not some kind of secret society are they?' She wasn't sure she liked the sound of all this.

Again Judy and Kate laughed. 'Guides? Secret? That's the last thing we are! There are thousands of us, all over the country. All over the *world!* One of the things we try hardest to do is to make friends with each other, and with everyone else we can,' Judy explained.

Kate interrupted her friend. 'Don't listen to Judy. She makes everything sound so *earnest.* Guides aren't like that. At least, we are about some things. But we have the most marvellous times too: picnics, and expeditions and parties, and so – it's so much *fun!* I'm sure you'd love it.'

Also in Beaver by Pamela Sykes

JULIET JOINS THE GUIDES

Pamela Sykes

BEAVER BOOKS

A Beaver Book

Published by Arrow Books Limited
62-65 Chandos Place, London WC2N 4NW

An imprint of Century Hutchinson Ltd

London Melbourne Sydney Auckland
Johannesburg and agencies throughout
the world

First published by Hodder & Stoughton 1984
Beaver edition 1986

Printed and bound in Great Britain by
Anchor Brendon Limited, Tiptree, Essex

ISBN 0 09 943110 6

For Juliet Pitman

who is *not* the 'Juliet' in this book,
but who helped to write it.

Contents

I

'Nothing to Do and No One to Do it With'

Dad, whose name was Mr Robertson, had always worked in a big city, so of course Mum, Juliet (who was just eleven) and Jimmie (who was nearly ten) had always lived in it.

One day, suddenly and unexpectedly, Dad's building firm moved out into the country, so he and his family moved too.

When Juliet and Jimmie were told what was to happen, neither was pleased.

'The country!' exclaimed Juliet, who knew nothing about the country. 'It'll be lonely and dull – we shan't know anybody there!' This was the kind of thing which worried Juliet. She was horribly shy.

'Why can't you get another job, Dad, so we don't have to move?' Jimmie asked. Unlike Juliet, he made friends easily, but didn't want to leave his old ones.

'Because new jobs are difficult to find,' said Dad. 'I'm lucky to have been given this one. There's a plan to build a big new housing estate, and anybody who's willing to move can stay with the firm. The others – well, they'll have to manage for work as best they can.'

Juliet went into the bathroom for a secret cry. Jimmie went for a long walk by himself. Mum said little, but Juliet, who was a very noticing person, guessed that Mum wasn't too happy either, though she said, briskly: 'Come along, then. We'd all better get ready for the move.'

So one spring day the Robertson family found itself in a cottage in a village. Their new home was very unlike their old one. That had been one of a line of red brick houses, all joined together, and very similar. Each had a tiny strip of garden at the back, a few shrubs at the front, matching gates, and front doors with numbers.

The cottage they moved into was built with grey stone, and was one of a cluster, built higgledy-piggledy. They were surrounded by little gardens – some tidier than others. Though they were supposed to have numbers, nobody seemed to pay much attention to them. Instead they had names: 'Lilac Lodge', 'Stonewell' or 'The Old Forge'. The Robertson's was called 'Rose Cottage'. 'Though,' as Dad said sourly, 'it must just as well have been called "Weed Patch" and be done with it,' Indeed the garden was very overgrown and neglected.

'Though I don't know why he grumbles,' Jimmie said secretly to Juliet. 'After all, it's his fault we're here. Now he goes on and on about how he wishes we weren't.'

This was true. Dad was quite clearly not happy, which made him difficult to have around. It was all quite easy to understand, if you thought about it. His firm was here to build large new houses on what had for years been buttercup fields. Dad had never before been in charge of such a big project. It was very important for him that he should make a success of it. The people who lived in the village for years, were – understandably – upset. Most of them had already decided that they didn't like Dad's firm, or anyone connected with it, especially Dad himself, and his family. There were angry looks at the furniture van while it unloaded outside Rose Cottage, and groups of villagers muttered while they stared. Mum pretended not to notice. Dad scowled, but said nothing. Jimmie said, 'Let them goggle. Who cares? Anyone would think we *wanted* to live in their rotten village.'

Juliet, like Mum and Dad, said nothing, but she minded quite terribly. It was bad enough to have to leave her old life in the city without being made to feel like an enemy as soon as she arrived in the country. Also she worried about Dad. They'd always been such good friends till now, but suddenly they didn't seem to be friends any longer. After his long day's work organising as foreman on the site, he was always tired and usually irritable. He'd eat his tea and then either gaze at television or read the paper. He didn't seem to want to talk, even to Juliet. Soon nobody wanted to talk to *him* because he always seemed ready for an argument, even if there was no need of one.

Mum never had a moment to spare because she was so busy trying to fit their furniture into different-shaped rooms, altering curtains, unpacking china, and generally trying to make things comfortable for everyone.

She told Juliet and Jimmie to leave their father in peace. 'Things are difficult for him at work,' she told them. 'He doesn't want to be bothered at home as well.'

Jimmie said 'I'm not going to bother him, don't worry. Old cross-patch!'

Mum said 'Tch! Tch!' but Jimmie didn't listen. Within twenty-four hours of arriving, he'd become friendly with a boy his own age called Steve. Perhaps it was because Juliet had always got on so well with her brother that she now found it difficult to take to Steve. She suddenly found herself left out of things. It was partly because Steve was one of those people who said things straight out loud, before he'd thought about it, and the things he said didn't always please Juliet. Or because the two boys were always out together, and generally came home late, tired, hungry and grubby.

Mum didn't fuss about this. 'As long as they're safe and happy,' she said. 'And it keeps them from getting under my feet.'

It was Juliet who seemed to be under Mum's feet all the time. She moped and sulked and grumbled till even her placid mother lost her temper. 'For goodness sake try to cheer up a bit!'

'There's nothing to cheer up *about*.'

'There would be if you looked for it. I know you're a bit on the shy side, love. But you must stop hanging about and looking miserable. We've all got to make an effort to get ourselves settled. Why can't you try to enjoy yourself, like Jimmie?'

'Because I'm not *like* Jimmie,' Juliet snapped. 'I've got nothing to do, and no one to do it with.'

'I can find you plenty to do, if that's the trouble,' Mum said, with a meaning look at a tray of newly-unpacked cups and saucers which all needed a good wash after their journey.

Juliet saw the look. 'You needn't bother,' she

said quickly. 'You're always saying there's not enough space in this kitchen for two, anyway.'

'There's hardly room for *one* in your bedroom,' said Mum sharply. 'It's almost impossible to open the door because of the junk inside. For goodness sake finish unpacking properly, and put everything away. I can't think how you can bear to live in such a disgusting state. I'd offer you the use of the vacuum if I thought there was a square foot of bare floor where you could use it. As it is, until you've sorted some of the clutter . . .' Juliet moved towards the door. 'If you really want to make yourself useful . . .' But she was already half way up the stairs. She managed, with some difficulty, to sidle into her bedroom. Looking round it, she had to admit to herself that Mum had a point.

Various garments still trailed half-in and half-out of her suitcase. The bed was unmade. Under it were several assorted shoes, most of them muddy. The wardrobe door swung open, but there wasn't much in it yet. There were some dusty shelves but the books and ornaments they should have held were lost in the tangle of tights and underclothes. The waste-paper basket lay on its side, surrounded by plastic bags, yellowing magazines, some apple-cores and a couple of coke tins. In fact, Mum had been absolutely right to describe the room as being in a 'disgusting' state.

Juliet sank on to the ruckled sheets of her bed and stared for a long time at the mess before she could make herself do anything about it. She saw the end of a coat-hanger sticking out from under a pair of levis. At last she made herself scrabble around until she found her one tidy dress, and hang it in the wardrobe. Then she flopped down again. What did it matter? There was nothing to wear the dress *for*, anyway!

In her wanderings round the village she'd passed a number of the children. They'd naturally stared at her with curiosity. But Juliet had also imagined that they had been sneering at her, not only because she spoke differently from them, but, more importantly, because her Dad was foreman of the builders who were spoiling their village. That wasn't fair, because it wasn't *her* fault, it was Dad's.

She was listlessly putting garments into different piles when Mum appeared.

'Good,' she said. 'You've made a start. Well done! Better get it all straightened out as soon as you can. Don't forget that term begins next week. You won't have so much time to yourself then. Why don't you have a break before you do the rest? I've just taken a fresh sponge out of the oven. Come on down and have the first slice.' She smiled so kindly that Juliet could hardly bear it.

'O.K. Mum,' she answered in rather a muffled

voice, and her head turned away. 'I'll be down in a minute.' Mum tactfully vanished. But Juliet couldn't move. Although she managed not to cry, she could hardly make her legs move, downstairs or anywhere else.

School!

Of course she'd always known she'd have to make a start at the big local comprehensive, but somehow she'd managed to bury the knowledge deep in the back of her mind, in spite of Dad having created about her need of a whole new uniform. At the time she'd only thought resent-fully 'I wouldn't have needed a new uniform if you hadn't made me leave my old school'. Almost at once she'd felt a beast even having *thought* like that. Poor Dad, he was having to be brave as well, and start work in a new place, and in a higher position than he'd ever held in the firm. But it would have been so nice if he'd even said, 'Sorry, this is going to be tough on you too, Julietta,' (only *he* was allowed to use that pet name). 'Best of luck.'

But he hadn't.

It was all right for Jimmie. For one thing he'd be one of the elder boys in the Junior School, instead of one of the younger ones, as she would be, in hers. For another, he'd made a friend of Steve, who was already there, and anyhow Jimmie never cared about what people thought.

Mum called, 'Come on down, Juliet!'

Her hand was damp on the banister as she clutched it on her way to the kitchen. She knew Mum was watching her as she ate, so she tried to be ordinary, although the cake, usually her favourite, nearly choked her.

In the next few days she felt worse and worse. She knew her feelings showed, because she occasionally heard the odd word when Mum and Dad were talking about her.

Mum: '. . . she's bound to find it hard at first.' Dad: '. . . moody . . . spoilt . . .' Mum: '. . . you must be patient with her . . .' Dad: 'If Jimmie can cope without all this sulking . . .' Mum: 'She and Jimmie are quite different . . .' Juliet hated to think that she was the cause of Mum and Dad arguing in a way which they never used to.

Suddenly it was the first day of term. Juliet felt funny in her new uniform. She had an odd pain at breakfast, but she had said nothing about it, in case they thought she was only putting it on. In the bus there were rows of faces she didn't know. It was worse when they got there. Somebody kind showed her the cloakrooms, her peg, her locker, and her classroom. One girl and two boys made remarks and asked her name. Her mouth was so dry with shyness that she could hardly give it, which made her sound, she was sure, stuck up and unfriendly.

The most difficult time was the morning

break. Of course there must have been other new girls there besides herself, but Juliet didn't know which they were. She hoped they weren't feeling as left out as she was. Naturally there was lots of chatter, because the pupils came from miles around to this school, and everybody wanted to catch up on other people's news. As Juliet had no one to talk to, she stood alone. She found herself near a group of much bigger boys than she had ever had to face at her previous school. Of course she didn't know their names, but there seemed to be a Wayne and a Bill, Mike, Geoff and several others.

Juliet said nothing, but she watched carefully. Wayne was showing the others something small and bright blue. She couldn't see what it was, but heard one of the other boys exclaim: 'A book of pocket matches with your *own* initials on it. I say, that's quite *something*!'

Wayne looked smug, and another boy peered more closely and said: 'W. W. for Wayne Wilson, in *gold* too! I wish I had a rich friend who worked in clubs and could get me things like that on the side.'

Wayne laughed and said, 'It's only a matter of knowing the right people!'

When the admiring was over, the boys felt in their pockets, and huddled closer. Wisps of grey smoke rose from the group.

Smoking! Juliet realised. How *stupid*! Didn't

they know it would very likely kill them? She knew what Mum and Dad thought about smoking, and why. But of course she kept quiet.

Suddenly one of the big boys said, 'Look, there's a kid hanging about, spying.'

All the others whipped round and stared at Juliet. 'One word about this and you'll be sorry. Who are you, anyway?'

Another boy said, 'I know who she is. Her dad's the one that's mucking up the buttercup fields with horrid little houses.'

'Oh, *is* she?' said Bill, and Juliet wished she were a hundred miles away.

Mike – or was it Geoff? – said, 'Hmph! We can do without any of *that* lot! Ruining our village!'

'Better than ruining your *health*, anyway!' Juliet retorted, before she could help it. Then she hastily got out of the way.

At tea-time, when Mum asked her questions, she tried not to answer because she didn't want her to know how unhappy she was. Jimmie chattered away about his own school day. He seemed perfectly cheerful. Juliet envied him, especially when she overheard Dad saying to Mum. 'That girl's sulking again. What's wrong with her?'

Mum said quickly, 'Nothing, she's tired that's all. She'll get used to it. Just give her time.'

A few days later, during break, two girls came

up to her, as she was standing alone and secretly longing for the bell for lessons to ring. 'Hello,' said one. 'I'm Kate. This is Judy. You're Juliet Robertson aren't you?' Juliet admitted, nervously, that she was.

'Then you were the one that answered back when the big boys tried to bully you,' said Judy admiringly. 'You must be brave.'

'I'm not a *bit*!' said Juliet. 'Ever. I just spoke without thinking.'

'I'm like that, too,' said Kate, 'I don't seem to be able to help it sometimes. Isn't that true, Judy?' Judy nodded, apparently not at all insulted as Kate went on: 'although she's calmer, she's quite, quite scatty – you know, forgetting or losing things all the time.'

'True, I'm afraid,' said Judy ruefully. 'But you were quite right to stand up to those idiots. They only do stupid things to show off. Most of their friends from Belton – that's the nearest village to ours – have left, you see. They don't have much sense, either. Most of them have motor bikes and they all wear red helmets and ride fast – too fast – around here, and sneer at Wayne and his lot who are still at school. So there's a sort of gang war all the time.'

'Daft, I call it,' said Kate.

'Me too,' agreed Judy. 'I say, would you like to come back to tea after school one day?'

Juliet was not used to sudden invitations, let

alone accepting them. 'Are you sure?' she asked.

'Of course I am, stupid, or I wouldn't have asked you!' said Judy.

Juliet didn't mind being called 'stupid', because she knew it was said in a friendly, not unkind way. 'Thanks,' she said. 'I'd love to.' She found, to her surprise, that she would.

'And you must come to me sometimes,' Kate added.

Mum was delighted when she heard of the invitations. 'There! I knew you'd find some friends in the village soon.' She was glad to hear they both lived nearby. 'Good. Then you can walk home. But while it's still daylight mind. Don't forget.'

'I won't,' Juliet promised. Mum had always been very strict about her not being out alone in the dark.

Of course as soon as the day came, Juliet began to wish she hadn't agreed to go out to tea. Suppose she did something wrong? Or said something that sounded silly or forgot her manners in some way?

None of these things happened. Judy's mum, Juliet discovered, was very like her own, and so was the rest of the family, the youngest of whom, Thomas, was not yet two. Just at first everyone talked rather politely, but soon they were all laughing and chatting as if they'd known each other for years. After tea, (which included a lovely omelette, and little iced sponge-cakes) Judy took Juliet up to her room to show her some photographs.

Juliet was amazed by the bedroom. It was as neat and as clean as a new pin. There was not so much as an old tissue or a slightly grubby comb to be seen. How impressed Mum would have been! Juliet thought of her own room with shame. She would certainly have to do something more about that before Judy came to *her*!

'I wish my room was as tidy as yours,' she couldn't help exclaiming.

'Is it a mess?'

'Fearful,' Juliet admitted.

'Never mind. Mine used to be the same,' said Judy. 'But when –' she suddenly stopped, rather mysteriously. 'But it's better now,' she finished, though Juliet was sure she was about to have said something different.

'How did it go?' Mum asked as soon as Juliet got home.

'Great,' Juliet admitted. 'It was almost like being at home.'

Mum looked pleased. 'I'm so glad you enjoyed yourself, love. You must ask her back sometime.'

'Thanks, Mum. I'd like to.'

'And I'll ask Steve the same day,' Jimmie put in. 'We'll make up a foursome. He's got some new tapes. I'll get him to bring them.'

Juliet wondered if she wanted to have Jimmie and Steve around the first day Judy came. Mum also evidently had doubts, but of a different kind. 'We don't want a lot of noise,' she warned. 'You know your father needs peace and quiet when he gets home.'

'Oh him!' exclaimed Jimmie. 'This is our *home* isn't it?'

'As long as he can pay for it,' said Mum. 'Don't forget that.'

Juliet looked doubtfully at her mother. 'Sure it'll be all right?'

'Of course it will, as long as you keep the sound down a bit.' She seemed very matter-of-fact, but Juliet wondered now how matter-of-fact she really felt. It didn't do to ask though. Mum had always had a way of keeping her feelings private. She, too, must have noticed the change in Dad. But as she never mentioned it, Juliet didn't either.

However, the tea-party was a success, and the following week Juliet went to tea with Kate, and Judy was included in the invitation. So she found herself with two new friends. This cheered her up, and also made school easier.

Until a few days later, as everyone was getting ready to go home, Juliet saw Kate and Judy talking. She was close by. Judy looked up and saw her. Instantly she gave Kate a nudge. Only a little one, but Juliet noticed it. At once their conversation stopped. It was only too obvious that they had been talking about her. Juliet felt cold all over. She walked quickly away, her new feeling of happiness gone. On the way home she worried and wondered. What had they been saying about her that they didn't want her to hear? Perhaps they'd only asked her to their homes to find out what she was like out of school, and had been disappointed. And yet everything had seemed to go well. Where had she gone wrong?

She was so troubled by her doubts that she accidentally bumped into a little old lady, being tugged along by a small dog.

To be more accurate the dog bumped into *her*. He clearly wanted to go in one direction, whilst the frail owner was trying to persuade him to go in another.

Somehow Juliet got mixed up in this disagreement. The old lady cried 'Oh! – I'm *so* sorry!' as the dog bounded at Juliet, who landed in a very cold wet ditch.

2

Trouble

'I'm *so* sorry!' stammered Juliet, scrambling out of the ditch, and hoping she wasn't as smelly as she felt she was. 'I wasn't looking where I was going.'

'Don't worry, my dear,' said the old lady. 'It was as much our fault as yours. Tramp is so strong that I sometimes feel that *he* takes *me* for walks, rather than the other way round!'

'Can I stroke him?' Juliet asked.

'Of course, my dear. He wouldn't hurt a fly.'

Juliet bent to fondle Tramp because she liked

dogs, but had been unable to have one of her own. The old lady said, 'I'm Mrs Mitchell. I think you live just round the corner, don't you?'

Juliet thought she'd better get it all over at once. 'Yes. I'm Juliet Robertson. It's my dad that's in charge of the new estate. I'm awfully sorry if you hate it all, like every one else does, but it's not his fault, and –'

'Of course it's not,' said the old lady, calmly but surprisingly. 'Somebody's got to see about it. I've lived in the village all my life –' (Juliet felt more awful) '– and I loved the buttercup meadows as much as anyone. George – that's my husband who's passed on – and I did our courting there. Those were hard times, but it's harder still now for young people to set up home. They've got to live somewhere, haven't they? Oh, I know there's some who are upset, but I'm not one of them.'

Juliet was astonished. This dear little old lady, who had actually 'done her courting' in the buttercup fields, didn't hate Dad, or anyone in his family. She felt warm inside. Then she had a sudden idea.

'Mrs Mitchell, if Tramp is too strong for you, would you like – I mean – I don't want to butt in – but you see, I love dogs, and –' she finished in a rush – 'would you like me to take him out for you sometimes?'

Mrs Mitchell beamed. 'Now that's very kind.

All this talk about the young being selfish – I've always said –'

By the end of the conversation it had been arranged that Juliet would go round to Honeysuckle Cottage, Mrs Mitchell's home, and take Tramp for a walk each day after school. Everybody was pleased by the arrangement, especially, it seemed, Tramp, who leapt up to try to lick Juliet's face.

'Come and see me, any day, my dear,' said Mrs Mitchell, 'I don't meet many young people.'

'I'd like to,' Juliet said, meaning it.

For a moment after she had walked, or rather been tugged, into her cottage by Tramp, Juliet felt a glow of warmth. She'd made a real friend, she was certain. Two, counting Tramp.

Then she remembered how Judy and Kate had whispered behind her back and the glow faded. Of course she was still glad to have made a friend, but very sad about having apparently lost two others.

The next morning at school was difficult, because she dreaded coming face to face with Kate or Judy, in case they ignored her, or started whispering again. Once when she saw them coming towards her, she turned quickly and walked in the opposite direction. She thought she heard Judy call her name, but deliberately pretended not to hear. They probably only wanted to say something to patch things up, but

Juliet didn't want the kind of friendships which needed patching up. It might easily be, she decided, a case of 'two's company, three's none'. So she kept out of their way.

It was a surprise, therefore, when they cornered her at the end of the afternoon.

'Look here,' said Kate bluntly. 'What's going on? You've been avoiding us all day. Why?'

The question was so unexpected that for a moment Juliet didn't know how to answer it. Then she decided to be completely honest. 'You were talking about me in the cloakroom yesterday. I know you were, because you stopped as soon as you saw me.' She felt hot and uncomfortable, but was determined to go on. 'I thought you wanted to be friends, but if you are going to whisper about me behind my back, I don't want to know.'

To her surprise, they both laughed. 'We *were* talking about you!' said Judy. 'We were only being quiet because we didn't want everyone to hear.'

'Especially me,' Juliet could not help putting in.

'Not then,' Kate agreed, 'but we do now. You see, we're both Guides, and we were agreeing that you were just the right kind of person to be one too, and wondering if you'd like us to suggest it.'

Perhaps Juliet looked a little blank, because

Kate went on. 'You must know about Guides?'

Juliet remembered vaguely seeing older girls in the city wearing smart blue uniforms, sometimes in church or on parade, or doing various things here and there. 'Not much,' she had to admit.

'Then it's time you did,' said Kate firmly. 'And we want to tell you.'

Juliet frowned. 'They're not some kind of secret society are they?' She wasn't sure she liked the sound of all this.

Again Judy and Kate laughed. 'Guides? Secret? That's the last thing we are! There are thousands of us, all over the country. All over the *world*! One of the things we try hardest to do is to make friends with each other, and with everyone else we can,' Judy explained.

Kate interrupted her friend. 'Don't listen to Judy. She makes everything sound so *earnest*. Guides aren't like that. At least, we are about some things. But we have the most marvellous times too: picnics, and expeditions and parties, and so – it's so much *fun*! I'm sure you'd love it.'

Juliet remained doubtful. 'I'm not very good at meeting new people, so –'

'– so all the more reason for joining!' said Judy.

Kate delved into her satchel. 'Look, I've brought this to lend you so that you can find out all about them.' She produced a blue and gold paperback book named 'The Guide Hand-book'.

'But – but – I'm not sure that I *want* to be a Guide!'

'You will be, when you know more about them,' Judy promised. 'We have terrific fun.'

Kate pushed the Handbook at Juliet. 'Come on. Give it a chance.'

Juliet looked from Judy's eager face to Kate's. There was no doubt about it – they were still her friends, and even wanted to include her in what was clearly their favourite activity.

'Okay,' she said casually. She didn't want them to see how pleased she was, though she had a feeling they'd guessed.

At home she managed to have a quick peek into the book from time to time. The more she read, the more interested she became. She discovered that Guiding took up time, and also, Kate and Judy warned her, a little money. She knew Dad's feelings about *that* at the moment. Juliet thought she'd better have a word with Mum before deciding anything, and as soon as the two of them found themselves privately in the kitchen, she took the opportunity.

'Guides?' said Mum. 'I know I ought to but I'm afraid I don't know a lot about them.'

'Nor do I, yet,' Juliet admitted, 'but Kate lent me a book about them and I must say the Guides seem to have fun, although they do hard work too. But she and Judy say they have a *marvellous* time, so they think I might like to join.'

Mum had been damping down clothes for ironing. She paused, with a shirt in her hand. 'I'm glad that you're going to join in with something in the village, but –'

'I didn't say I was *going* to,' Juliet interrupted quickly, 'but I *think* I'd like to. That is, if –' she hesitated.

'If what?' asked Mum. She seemed to have forgotten about the shirt.

Juliet went on with difficulty. 'If – you see, the thing is, I have to have my parents' permission before I can join.'

'I *do* see,' said Mum. She paused, '*Both* parents?'

'Well, I'm not sure. I suppose if you didn't actually *have* a dad – I mean, have two parents – one would do – but –'

'Tell me more about what it would mean. I know a *little* about Guides of course, but if *you* were one, what would you have to do?'

'Oh, an awful lot,' Juliet said. 'I haven't read much of the book yet, but they seem to get up to all sorts of things, but you have to try to behave as well – don't smile, Mum, I saw you! I do try. But it looks as if I'm going to have to try a bit harder.'

'That's the good news, anyhow,' said Mum. 'Go on.'

'It's not all difficult. There are meetings and camp holidays and parties and projects, and badges you can work for – Oh, heaps of things which sound great. I'm almost *sure* I'd like to join. But I must find out a bit more first.'

'That makes sense,' said Mum. She turned away to attend to the shirt again, so that she wasn't looking at Juliet. 'One more point. No one gets anything for nothing these days. If you *do* decide to join the Guides, how much will it cost?'

Juliet was silent, reckoning. 'First I ought to have my own Guide Handbook. Then, if I can do all I have to, I'll need a uniform. I'm not sure how much that would cost. Not much, I think, but I know it all adds up. And if we – that is, the Guides get together and do things, everyone pays a little bit –'

She saw Mum's face, though she was now busy with Jimmie's pyjamas. 'Not much,' said Juliet quickly, 'and perhaps I could earn some of it –'

'Let's hope so,' Mum said, suddenly brisk again. 'Everybody has to help with expenses these days. In the meantime –' she paused. Juliet knew why. 'I shouldn't mention it to Dad if I were you, till you're sure. I'll find the right moment and have a word.' She rolled up the pyjamas and started on another shirt. 'If you really want to be helpful you could put the

bacon-and-egg pie into the oven, get the potatoes on and lay the table.'

Juliet left it at that. Mum understood. Somehow she'd make things come right. She always
did. Juliet sorted out the pie, the potatoes and laid
the table tidily. She stood back to see if there was
anything she'd forgotten. Salt, sugar, bread and
butter, cheese, pickles , spring cabbage ready to
cook. She would take Mum's hint and not mention Guides. With any luck, this evening might
go well.

It didn't. Jimmie was only just home in time
for tea, and extremely grubby.

Dad pounced on him immediately. 'Just *look* at
you! Go and get cleaned up at once. There's mud
all over your sweater, and that only new for
school.'

Jimmie knew the signs of a storm approaching
as well as anyone else did. He scuttled off towards the bathroom.

'And don't take all the hot water!' his father
shouted after him. 'I might even need some
myself!'

The storm broke during tea. Dad, who had
been grimly quiet, suddenly thumped his fist on
the table cloth so hard that his tea slopped on the
clean white cloth. Very briefly, Juliet met her
mother's eye. More washing, more ironing,
they both thought. And more trouble.

'I don't know what's wrong with this place!'

Dad exploded. 'If I'd had any sense I'd never have come here!'

Mum, Juliet and Jimmie, who had all found the move from their old house a hard one, said nothing, till Mum said soothingly. 'You were quite right to come here, Fred. Don't you remember telling me how you'd have lost your job if you hadn't? How's the work going?'

'It'd be going a d——,' Dad checked himself, 'a great deal better if the local louts kept away from the site!'

'Local louts?' Mum queried.

'Vandals!' shouted Dad. 'When I got there this morning there was "GO AWAY, WE DON'T WANT YOU HERE" in bright green paint – still sticky – written on the cement-mixer. It's enough to make you sick!'

Juliet felt sorry for Dad. At first, going to a new school had been enough to make her sick, too. She understood how he felt. All the same, she hadn't made a big Thing of it, like Dad was doing now. She longed for the Dad she used to know. Of course he'd had his snappy moments (who didn't?) but he'd never been like this.

Before she could get a word in, Mum said, 'I wouldn't take any notice, Fred. It's only a few hooligans, with more time than sense.'

'Hmph!' Dad snorted. 'If you ask me, there's not a soul in this benighted place who wouldn't be glad to see the back of us.'

'Oh, *no*!' Juliet exclaimed before she could stop herself. 'There is a soul, Dad, honestly.'

Dad's thick eyebrows became closer to each other as he glared at her. 'And what do *you* know about it, I may ask?'

'Not very much, but I do know one person who thinks the new houses are a good thing. That's old Mrs Mitchell.'

'And who's Mrs Mitchell when she's at home?' Dad's tone was threatening.

'She's a nice little old lady. And she almost *is* at home, because she lives next door at "Honeysuckle Cottage". I've arranged to take Tramp – that's her dog – out for walks because he's too strong for her and –'

'I don't want to hear about any dog,' growled Dad, sounding rather like an angry dog himself. 'What's the old busybody been saying to you? That's what I'd like to know?'

Juliet knew that Jimmie was gaping at her, and Mum was wearing a warning expression, but she went on. 'She's not a "busybody". She's a dear. And she's lived in the village all her life. She and George – that's her husband who's passed on – did their courting in the buttercup fields, but even *she* says, "Young people have got to have *somewhere* to live." So she's pleased about the new houses!'

'Great', said Dad in not at all a nice voice. 'One barmy old woman thinks the development's a good idea. That makes my day, that does.'

'She's not barmy at all,' Juliet answered hotly. 'And it's not my fault, or hers, if what she thinks doesn't make your day.'

She could see the faces Mum was making at her, and that Jimmie's eyes were round. She was suddenly even more afraid of her own boldness.

'Did I ask your opinion?' Dad asked her in a fierce voice.

'No, but I thought you'd like to know –'

'Then you can stop thinking,' said Dad. 'I know all I need to know, and that is that some-body's got it in for us!'

'Don't go on about those hooligans,' said Mum. 'It's not just *you* they're against. Look how they smashed up the telephone kiosk last week. They keep doing it, people tell me, every time it's mended. People seem to think it's a group of No-goods from Belton.'

'Fat lot of help *thinking* is,' muttered Dad. 'I can tell you one thing. Whoever's responsible for this, I'm going to sort them out!' He attacked his pie fiercely, and nobody spoke.

Several days passed. Juliet took Tramp for walks on each of them, and then popped in to have a cup of tea and a chat with Mrs Mitchell. But it was evident that Mum had not yet found the right moment to put in a word with Dad about Guides. There certainly didn't seem to *be* a right moment, and most of the words put in were used by Dad. Some of them were words that Juliet and Jimmie were not allowed to use.

There came an evening when Jimmie and Steve were out. 'Making a map of the village for geography,' Jimmie called it. 'Skiving off proper homework,' Dad called it, 'or else schools have gone even more mad than I'd thought.' All the same, it had been steak and kidney pie for tea – his favourite – and when the boys had gone, Mum gave Juliet a special look as she said: 'Be a dear and see to the washing-up for me will you?'

Juliet understood the look, and at least she already knew that the second of the Guide Laws was 'Guide is helpful', so she went off quickly to the kitchen. She made the washing-up last for as long as possible, which was not difficult, as the pastry had stuck to the rim of the pie-dish and needed a lot of scraping off. Even after she'd put everything carefully away and laid the table for breakfast, she could still hear the sound of voices from the sitting-room. Dad's voice was louder than Mum's. It sounded like another argument. Oh dear. Was it *all* because of her? She felt guilty.

One thing was certain. She would not be welcome in the sitting-room at this moment. So, just in *case* things turned out all right after all, she crept upstairs and brought Kate's Handbook into the kitchen. At first she only flipped through the pages.

But soon she became fascinated.

3

More Trouble

In some vague way, Juliet had always thought of
Girl Guides – if she'd thought of them at all – as
being rather old-fashioned. The more she read of
the Handbook, the more she realised how wrong
she had been. She was amazed to find how
grown-up and responsible they were supposed
to be, though the Handbook thought that *enjoying* yourself was important too!

She was interested to discover you could work
for an Artist's Badge, because she'd always loved
drawing and painting and now discovered there
were lots of ways in which one could put the

talent to good use. She'd been saving up to buy herself a new paintbox for some time. Now she'd have a good excuse.

She was also pleased to find how necessary it was to be able to remember accurately, and be a noticing person, because she knew she was good at both those things.

By now she knew of course, that the Guide motto was 'Be Prepared' but when she read the list of things she would be encouraged to learn, she was really impressed. She was still reading when Jimmie and Steve crashed in through the back door, complete with note-book and pencils. They were surprised to see her in the kitchen.

'What's going on?' asked Jimmie.

'Sssh!' said Juliet. 'Mum and Dad are having a – a – talk.'

'*Oh!*' said Jimmie knowingly.

'I expect you mean having a row,' said Steve, in his outright way. 'Don't fuss, our Mum and Dad are always having rows. Funny how *they* can argue, but we're not allowed to, isn't it?'

Juliet didn't think it was funny. 'How did your mapping go?' she asked quickly.

'So – so,' said Steve. 'We couldn't do the bit round the Memorial Cross. That beastly lot from Belton were there swanking about their bikes. I saw one of them throw something at a cat,' he added with disgust.

'How foul,' said Juliet. The more she heard about the Belton gang the less she liked the sound of them.

'Wayne, and one or two others from our side were there,' Steve told her. 'It looked as if there was going to be another fight so we – we – came away.'

Juliet couldn't honestly blame them for that, but when Jimmie asked hopefully, 'Any chance of a sandwich?' she said 'No,' very firmly. 'I've cleared everything away and washed the floor, and *look* at your shoes!'

'You sound just like Mum,' complained Jimmie. But he took his shoes off, and said to Steve, 'It's beginning to get dark. Do you think you ought to be getting home?'

'What you really mean is that you want to get rid of me,' said Steve cheerfully. 'You're right though, I'll probably get into trouble as it is.'

He took himself and his homework and his muddy shoes away.

Jimmie shut the door quietly. 'Trouble here too?' he whispered.

Juliet nodded. 'And I probably started it off.' She held up the Handbook.

'Are you sure it's worth it?'

Only a few minutes ago, Juliet would have said. 'I'm not sure.' Now, because she felt Jimmie was trying to put her off Guides, she suddenly wanted very much to be one.

'Yes,' she said firmly. 'I'm going up to bed.' she added.

'This early?'

'I know, but we can't go in *there*, so we can't watch telly. Anyway I haven't even started my homework. I'd keep out of the way, if I were you.'

Upstairs she did do her homework, rather sketchily, and then went back to the Handbook. She'd read all she could, she decided, before she finally made up her mind.

A long time later, she realised it was past the time when she was supposed to have put her light out. Bother! Just as she was getting really interested. For a moment she hesitated. The light would show under the door, but she must read some more. Although what she was about to do had always been strictly forbidden, Juliet crept out of bed, eased a drawer open quietly, and took out her torch.

She flicked out the light and was presently reading under the bedclothes. She was so absorbed, wondering whether it would be more fun to go on an exploring camp, or help to paint the scenery for a pantomime, that she didn't hear the footsteps on the stairs. Or the door quietly opening.

'*What do you think you're doing?*'

Juliet was so startled that she gave a jump, and

the torch, still lit, rolled from under the bed-clothes across the floor.

The light snapped on. Dad stood in the door-way. He was furious.

Juliet could only struggle to sit up. There was nothing she could possibly say.

Dad looked at the torch. 'You *know* you're not allowed to strain your eyes like that! How many times have we told you? Have you any idea what the time is? Five to eleven! What were you reading?'

Juliet had to produce Kate's Handbook.

Dad snatched it from her. 'Guides! I might have known! There was your mother telling me how much good it would do you to be one – She'd almost got me to agree, but I know better now! Even reading the book has made you disobedient and deceitful. Well you can forget about the wretched Guides, because I'll see to it you never are one!'

He went out slamming the door behind him.

After Dad had gone, Juliet rescued the torch, put out the light, huddled into bed, and cried dreadfully. How *could* she have been so stupid, just when she had decided she really *did* want to be a Guide? And at the very time when Mum was trying to persuade Dad it would be a good idea, she'd deliberately misbehaved.

Worse, in doing so, she'd broken another Guide Law – which was: 'A Guide had to promise, among other things to be trustworthy and obedient.' She'd been neither.

Anyway, she thought drearily, she'd never would be a Guide. Dad would see to that. And she really couldn't blame him. For once he had a reason to be angry, and she had no one to blame but herself.

Next morning, though she had washed her face in cold water, it was still obvious from her red swollen eyes that she'd been crying. Breakfast was almost a silent meal, except for remarks like, 'Would you like another cup of tea?' or 'Butter, please'. Nobody discussed openly the goings on of the night before, though after Dad had left for work, Mum said reproachfully, 'You were silly, love. And after I'd almost talked him round. Never mind. Try not to think about it. You never know what might happen.'

Juliet was sure she *did* know what would happen: more trouble.

While she and Jimmie, who'd heard the rumpus, were frantically sorting their satchels, he hissed. 'You're a first class twit!'

By the time she got to school, having been coldly ignored by Dad, described as 'silly' by Mum and a 'first class twit' by Jimmie, and full of her own private unhappiness, Juliet was in a very bad state. Her efforts to hide this were not successful. Nobody actually *said* anything, but Juliet knew, from sideways looks, nudges and whispered comments that people were talking about her.

When the morning break came, she wanted to hide, but as this was impossible, she did her best to seem ordinary. She failed. Through meeting Kate and Judy, Juliet had now become fairly friendly with other pupils. Some of them kept out of her way. Others made cheerful remarks, a few, realising that she was upset, tried to be kind. These were the most difficult to deal with, because – as most people know – if you are miserable and trying to hide it, kindness is the very thing which makes you want to start crying again.

She wandered about alone. It seemed as if the bell for lessons would never ring. Before it had, Judy came up to her. She was very direct. 'Juliet,' she said, 'what's the matter?'

'Nothing,' mumbled Juliet.

'Don't be an absolute idiot. Anyone can see there's something wrong. What is it? Come on, you'll feel better when you've told me.'

'I won't,' Juliet said. 'I'll feel worse – if that's possible.'

'Why?' Evidently Judy did some quick thinking. 'Is it to do with Guides?'

Juliet took a big breath. 'Yes. Everything's gone wrong. I can't be one.'

'Can't *be* one? Why ever not?'

'Dad said no.' Juliet saw Judy's expression.

'Please don't ask me about it. It's all my own fault. Anyway, I'd have made a rotten Guide. I know that now.'

'What nonsense!' exclaimed Judy. 'You'd make a wonderful one.'

The bell rang. 'We must go,' said Juliet hurriedly.

It wasn't so easy to escape in the dinner hour. Judy and Kate made it their business to talk privately to her.

'Look,' Kate said, 'we're your friends, we're not just being nosey. Honestly. But you said you can't be a Guide – something to do with your dad. If you told us about it, we could possibly help. And if we couldn't, Mrs Bailey, our Guider, could. I don't know how she does it, but she's marvellous at getting parents sorted out. Not just Guides. Parents as well. Honestly. If she explained to your dad –'

'Oh, *no*!' exclaimed Juliet. She thought of Dad in one of his moods being sorted out by this Mrs Bailey, a Guider. By *anyone*!

Judy was earnest. 'Truly. Juliet. I mean, all of us get into muddles at home sometimes. And you can tell her anything. Anything at all. And somehow it all comes right.'

Juliet shook her head. 'Not for me, it wouldn't, because Dad – no, that's not fair. It's not just him. It's me. You see . . .'

And somehow, in rather a jumbled fashion,

she told them the whole story. It was a great relief to tell it, though she was a little hurt when Kate and Judy laughed at her. Not unkindly, but in an understanding way.

'Juliet,' said Judy. 'Jimmie was right. You *are* a first class twit. There's no need to get in such a fuss. Anyone would think you were a *criminal*! Almost everybody gets caught reading with a torch in bed sometimes. It's *not* a good idea, because it *can* hurt your eyes. But I'll tell you one thing. At least you were reading something worthwhile.'

'Dad didn't think so,' said Juliet.

'Then your dad was wrong.'

'And another thing,' Juliet felt awful, but she had to say it, 'it was *your* Handbook, Kate, remember. He's got it, and I don't know whether he'll give it back.'

'Of course he will,' said Kate cheerfully. 'Mrs Bailey will see to that.'

'But I don't *want* Mrs Bailey to –'

'Oh, don't be such a donkey!' said Judy rudely. 'We know her and you don't. But you will. She only lives in the lane behind the school. We'll all go and see her this afternoon on our way home.'

'I *don't* know that I *want* to see her!' Juliet protested. But at that moment the bell rang again and the conversation had to end.

The afternoon was rather unexpected for

Juliet. Their homework had been to write an essay on the Common Market. Hers, as it had been rather scribbled off to make time for the Handbook (what a waste of time), was returned to her so that she could re-write it more neatly. She was not surprised.

What did surprise her that amongst several others, Kate and Judy got into trouble too. Kate was told she'd given far too little thought to the subject, and that if she'd read the newspapers more intelligently, she might – just *might* – know more about it.

Kate was heard to mutter something.

'*What* did you say?' demanded Miss Whitely, who was conducting the session.

Kate muttered again. Now everybody was listening.

'I beg your pardon?' asked Miss Whitely sarcastically, but still Kate wouldn't answer.

Juliet was amazed. Kate – a Guide! But not behaving in any of the ways that the Handbook had suggested she should.

Miss Whitely went on and on at Kate, who kept silent. Then, quite suddenly, words seemed to spout from her, so fast that not all could be heard. But from those which were, it was made clear from a now scarlet and defiant Kate that she thought the subject was dull and if she agreed with it okay, but if she didn't, what could she do about it, since she wasn't old enough to vote?

Anyway, things changed from day to day, and none of the papers said the same things, so what was the point of reading them. And –'

At this point, Miss Whitely, who had clearly had enough, said coldly. 'Thank you, Kate. We don't want to hear any more from you. Let's hope that *you* will never become our Prime Minister.'

'Hear, hear.' Kate agreed, and shut up.

Miss Whitely had various other comments to make on other peoples' essays, few of them complimentary. When she came to Judy, and asked 'And *where* might I ask is your paper?'

Judy looked abashed. 'Sorry,' she said. 'I did write one. But Thomas was cutting a tooth and howling so I cuddled him – Mum was ironing – so I couldn't get at the Common Market properly till I was in the bath. I'd nearly finished – that sponge thing that balances across, can be pretty handy – but suddenly it collapsed and I'm afraid all I've got left is –' and she held up a sodden mess of damp, stuck-together paper.

Miss Whitely was extremely displeased.

So, at last, the school day came to an end. Kate and Judy cornered Juliet in a very determined manner, in the changing-room. '*Now* –' they said. 'Off to Mrs Bailey – our Guider, remember? You said you would.'

'I *didn't*!' Juliet corrected. 'And anyway, how did you behave this afternoon? Not like *Guides*!'

'Not in the least,' Judy agreed calmly. 'But we do try,' she added quickly, 'though things don't always turn out right. So do *hurry* up!'

Somehow, Juliet found herself being hustled into her outdoor clothes, and off.

She didn't want to go a bit. She could guess what a Guider would be like. Single, elderly, well-meaning but boring – all the things Juliet felt she couldn't face up to. Or now – perhaps – even need to.

But Kate and Judy were determined not to let her off the interview. Without quite knowing how they managed it, Juliet found herself standing on Mrs Bailey's doorstep, Kate having rung the bell.

Juliet waited, with her heart in her (rather dirty) shoes.

4

'Nothing but Enjoying Yourselves'

Kate had to ring the bell four times, during which they heard sort of whirlwind noises.

At last Mrs Bailey appeared. She was not in the least like Juliet had expected.

She was quite young, and although there were the sounds of small children quarrelling, and the telephone chose that moment to ring, and you could tell from the smell that something had boiled over in the kitchen, she opened the door wide and said: 'Kate! Judy! Lovely to see you! And you've brought a friend! Better still! Come in – but you'll have to wait a minute – everything's happening at once.'

The others laughed at Juliet's surprised expression, as they took her firmly indoors.

'You see,' said Kate triumphantly. 'We *told* you –'

Certainly Mrs Bailey seemed to be good at sorting things out. She darted into the kitchen after which the smell wasn't quite so bad, and then answered the telephone very briskly, making notes as she did so. She then dealt firmly with her two little boys, and sent them into another room, and at the same time produced apparently from nowhere some chocolate biscuits, removed a few toys from the chairs and said, 'Sit down, you must be Juliet – Kate and Judy have told me about you – how can I help?'

It was all rather breath-taking. Although the problem was hers, the others did the talking, while Juliet listened. In no time at all Mrs Bailey seemed to know everything.

She turned to Juliet. 'We've been hoping you'll join the Company – you'd like to? Oh, *good*! Then we must see that you have the chance to prove it. Now then –' she paused, but only for a few seconds – 'you seem to have started off on the wrong foot at home. We'll have to put that right, of course. I think your father's the foreman at the new estate isn't he?'

'Yes,' said Juliet, wondering how Mrs Bailey knew.

'I've heard things aren't going too well. Some

people object to the whole scheme. Right?'

'Right,' Juliet agreed. 'In fact –' And in no time she found herself talking about Dad's difficulties and moods, including the painted slogans on the cement-mixer which she hadn't intended to mention. The others had been right. You could tell Mrs Bailey *anything*. It was quite difficult not to!

Rather to Juliet's surprise, she was very sympathetic about Dad. 'Poor man. What a dreadful time he's having. No wonder he's tired and worried by the time he gets home. You must realise, Juliet, that when people have troubles of their own, it's sometimes difficult for them to think clearly about other people's. Especially –' she looked hard at Juliet – 'if those other people don't behave sensibly.'

Juliet went red. She knew she had, but no one else appeared to notice. To change the subject, she said quickly. 'Dad thinks everyone's against him, and they're not.' Then she found herself talking about old Mrs Mitchell and her point of view, and then how she'd first met her and that she took Tramp for walks and did other little errands and jobs for her, and sometimes just sat and chatted.

'She's lonely you see,' Juliet explained. 'She likes to talk, especially about the old days. Sometimes I don't quite know what she's talking about, but I listen, anyway. She knows an awful lot about wild flowers. She told me once that she used to press them, and had filled a whole album, but it got thrown away. She's sad about that, because of the farmers spraying their crops. She says some of those flowers don't grow round here any more. Cowslips and some rare orchids, and –'

Suddenly Juliet realised that she was now doing all the talking, and thought she'd better stop. 'I'm sorry,' she said, going red again. 'I didn't mean to go on and on. I expect you're bored and –'

'Not bored at all,' said Mrs Bailey. 'Quite the reverse. I'm very glad to hear that you know dear old Mrs Mitchell, and that you're interested in wild flowers. And of course, she's right. We'll probably never see those flowers again round here, and it would have been so nice to have had a record of them. Or at least we could list all those that have escaped. But just don't pick anything and everything you see. There may still be some rare specimens left. Ask Mrs Mitchell to lend you a flower book with illustrations. I'm sure she'll have one, and be able to tell you the ones you can safely pick. If you should find something rare leave it alone, and tell us, and we might be able to help protect it.'

Suddenly the sound of the front door opening was heard – Mr Bailey coming home – and everyone realised with a jump how late it was, and stood up.

'Good gracious!' said Mrs Bailey. 'You must be on your way, or your parents will be worried. Thank you so much for coming. It's been lovely to meet you, Juliet, and don't worry. I'll have a word with your father.'

'Oh, please *don't*!' Juliet begged, but Kate and Judy muttered. 'Shut up! It'll be all right.' As they hurried out of the house Mr Bailey gave them a cheerful grin, as they passed, and the telephone rang again, and on the way home they wondered what time the little boys were supposed to go to bed, and if the tea Mr Bailey was expecting had been completely spoiled, and how on earth Mrs Bailey managed to do so many things at once and still be cheerful and kind and a Guider.

It was a few evenings later that she called at Juliet's home. Dad answered the door with a grim face. When Juliet saw who the caller was, she was so frightened that she ran upstairs. At the top of them she heard 'Good evening, Mr Robertson. You don't know me. My name's Ann Bailey. I hope you don't mind me calling, but I hear that there's been some trouble on your site. I know most of the people in this village, *and* the neighbouring ones, and I wondered if perhaps I could help to trace the offenders.'

Dad said, in a startled voice. 'Oh. Good of you. You'd better step in.'

Juliet didn't listen any more, but it was some

time before she heard Mrs Bailey leave. Both she and Dad sounded cheerful and polite and Juliet wondered what Mrs Bailey could have said to make Dad behave like that.

But one of Mrs Mitchell's father's favourite sayings had been 'Ask no questions, and you'll be told no lies', so Juliet asked no questions.

Next day Mum said, 'I've no doubt you know more than you'll admit, but that Mrs Bailey seemed to get on a treat with your dad. When she came and said it was about the vandals he was glad to have a moan about them. But by the time I went in they were talking about the Guide Movement and what a good thing it was. I wouldn't say anything to him if I were you, though. As a matter of fact,' she added carefully, 'I had a word with her myself. We – er – mentioned your bedroom, among other things.'

'You *didn't*!' gasped Juliet in horror.

'I did. She seemed interested. She *also* said she thought that *if* you join her Company, it would be a good idea for you to start keeping your room very tidy.'

'Oh,' said Juliet. There didn't seem to be anything else to say.

'I'll mention that to your dad; it might help. Remember he hasn't agreed to anything yet, but keep hoping.'

For the next few days, Juliet kept hoping, then, quite suddenly when she and Dad found themselves together in the garden, wondering what was growing in it, he said. 'That Mrs Bailey.'

It didn't seem to be a question so Juliet felt she didn't have to answer. She just held her breath. Dad said, after a pause, 'Seemed a sensible young woman.' Juliet said nothing. Dad said, pointing to some green spikes sticking out of the soil, 'Those look as if they might be daffodils.' He paused, and scratched his head. 'Or of course, they might not be.' Juliet still managed to keep silent.

'You didn't put her up to coming round, did you?' Dad asked suspiciously.

'No,' said Juliet, with truth. Then made herself ask, 'Why?'

'Because after a bit she was on about this Guiding lark you seem so keen on. Seems she is connected with it. She thought it would be a good thing if you joined.'

'Oh, *good*!' said Juliet.

'We'll have to see if it's good or not,' said Dad severely. 'She told me that it was possible to get second-hand uniforms, and that the whole thing needn't cost much, so I said we'd give it a try.'

Juliet was so pleased that she said, 'I think they *are* daffodils, Dad. Just think! Having them all free. We'd have to pay ever so much for them from a shop.'

'By the way, young Julietta,' said Dad. 'That

book of yours is in the right hand drawer of the dresser. But no more reading-in-bed nonsense. Understood?'

'Yes,' said Juliet. 'I promise. Thanks ever so much, Dad.'

'Better see if your mother wants a hand in the house,' said Dad gruffly.

Juliet, secretly *so* glad because he'd called her 'Julietta' again, almost danced into the house. She and Mum exchanged a secret smile.

So Juliet went to her first Guide meeting. She felt a bit odd, being the only one not to wear a uniform, but everyone made her feel so welcome that she soon forgot about it. Mrs Bailey explained that her company was divided into four Patrols, all named after birds: Swallows, Kingfishers, Wrens and Robins. Juliet was to be in Kingfishers, of which a tall girl called Christine was leader. Judy was in the same Patrol, and that made things fun, because sometimes the Patrols had little meetings on their own to make private plans, or to do useful things together, so Juliet knew she would soon get to know the other girls in her Patrol much better.

The work for that evening was about First-aid, and how to make do with anything you happened to have with you if an accident suddenly happened. This was something that Juliet had never thought about before. In a vague sort of way, she'd always imagined that if anyone were hurt or ill, Mum or Dad, or any other grown-up person would know what to do, and do it. Now, for the first time she realised that people of her own age could do a lot to help – and, what was more important, if you were a Guide you might be *expected* to! As there were several Guides working for their First Aid Badge, most of the evening was spent on the subject.

'After all,' said Mrs Bailey, 'whether you've decided to qualify for the Badge or not, the knowledge is always useful. The First Aid Badge is a Service Badge – such an important one that you must renew it every three years to make sure your knowledge is up to date, so it's a good idea for us *all* to know how to act in an emergency. Remember our Motto is "Be Prepared".'

Then she talked to the Company, answered questions, and discussed different situations. Juliet listened hard, but there was *so* much to learn! How to give mouth-to-mouth resuscitation; what was meant by 'shock' and how to deal with it; how to cope with scalds and cuts and injured limbs; how to bandage people properly and how to make do as best you could if there were no proper bandages at hand; possible causes of tummy-ache . . . and oh, so many other things that Juliet knew she would never remember all of them but she did her best.

During the last part of the meeting there was a session when people pretended to have something wrong with them, and other practised what they should do. At first one or two of the Guides tried to make a game of it and became a little giggly. At once Mrs Bailey seemed to become quite different. Instead of the easy-going, amusing person she had been till now, she turned into a strict Guider.

'That's enough of that,' she said sharply to the gigglers. 'We're not here to be childish, but to learn how to become responsible. One day you might find yourselves faced with a genuine emergency, or even suffer an accident your-selves. In either case, you'll then find out that the work you're supposed to be learning is no laughing matter.' That was all she said, but it was enough. Nobody played the fool any longer.

Juliet was amazed. She whispered to Judy. 'I didn't know she could be like that!'

'You do now,' Judy whispered back.

When they had finished bandaging one another up, and trying to remember how to do other things they'd been taught, they had a sing-song before the formal end of the meeting. As the evenings were getting longer, they were all able to walk safely home in the daylight.

The others made Juliet laugh about the good times they'd had, and how Mrs Bailey could be strict at one moment and not at all the next.

'Do you remember the time we had a cleaning-out-the-river-Saturday, and she fell into the water – *right* into it – and while we were still wondering which of us was going to save her life, she stood up, and laughed, so much, she could hardly speak –'

'And when she got hung upside-down in the apple tree just before Harvest Festival. I never knew Guiders wore red knickers –'

'But what about that concert which went so awfully wrong when the curtains wouldn't pull – ?'

'And the time –'

The other Guides started laughing so hard they could hardly walk.

'And the time –'

'Goodness!' exclaimed Juliet at last, 'you seem to have done nothing but enjoy yourselves.'

'Well, it can be rather hilarious,' Kate admitted, wiping her eyes. 'But we do work as *well*, like we did tonight, don't we?'

The only unpleasant part of the walk was when they passed the usual crowd of teenage boys hanging about in the square. Many of them had motor bikes and wore red helmets.

'Goody-Goody-Guides!' they chanted.

'Take no notice,' Judy whispered to Juliet. 'It's only the Belton gang.'

'Just pretend you haven't heard,' Kate said staring straight ahead while the boys shouted rude things at them.

'Go away! We don't want you here!' a voice yelled.

Juliet stopped walking. Suddenly.

'Get *on*!' Kate urged. 'They always hang about after Guide meetings just to annoy us.'

'*I* think that remark was meant 'specially for *me*,' Juliet said.

'He was saying it to *all* of us!' contradicted Judy. 'Don't imagine things.'

Juliet said no more. But she thought and she thought . . . and the more she thought the more certain she was that she was *not* imagining things.

Some time later it was time to think about *other* things, the most important of which was that Juliet and Mrs Bailey had arranged to have a talk about Juliet's Guiding work. They met at Mrs Bailey's house, where things seemed a little quieter and calmer than on Juliet's previous visit, and they discussed the eight Pre-Promise Challenges star, which stood for eight different kinds of ways by which Juliet could prove she was worthy to join the Guides.

Juliet sighed doubtfully at the eight headings in the Handbook.

'Cheer up!' said Mrs Bailey, 'they're not as difficult as they seem. Keeping the Guide Laws, we know you'll try to. Exploring the Arts. How do you feel about that?'

'I'm fond of painting,' said Juliet.

'Good,' said Mrs Bailey. 'But "exploring" means finding out about something you can't already do. Remember that acting and singing and dancing are "Arts" too.'

Juliet didn't actually wriggle her body, but she wriggled inside her head, because the forms of art which Mrs Bailey had mentioned all meant being watched and listened to, both of which Juliet hated.

Her Guider she knew was watching her. 'Very well,' she said. 'We'll leave that out for the moment. But if you find you can't suggest some way of accepting that challenge. I'll think of a way for you and expect you to do something about it. Do you understand? Right. Let's think of "Getting to know People". You must have got to know some people recently because you moved here from somewhere else.'

'Yes,' said Juliet. 'People at school, of course. I had to. And Kate and Judy, especially. Although to be honest it was they that made friends with *me*.' She saw Mrs Bailey was smiling and realised why. 'Because they were Guides I suppose!'

'That's right. They could see you were lonely and did what they could to help. And it was through them that you met me, and then the other Guides. You see how it works? Then there's Mrs Mitchell, of course. It was *you* that made friends with her. I know you do little jobs for her –' (How did Mrs Bailey know so much?) – 'And exercise Tramp, so you're both "Giving" and "Service" *and* "Keeping Fit". And are you enjoying "Out of Doors"?'

'More and more,' Juliet said, 'mostly because of the flowers.'

'Then there's "Home Maker" .'

Juliet went a little pink and Mrs Bailey laughed. 'So you know now why I had a chat with your mum about your bedroom. See that after you've *made* it tidy, you must *keep* it tidy. And clean. If you make a good job of that, I'll ask your mum to sign a paper to say that you have.'

'For how long?' asked Juliet.

'For *ever*, we hope!'

Juliet nearly said that if she succeeded in keeping her bedroom tidy and clean for even a week, Mum would probably die of shock and that would hardly be Giving Service to the rest of the family, but it was not the moment to be funny so she didn't try. But she had a sudden thought as she remembered Judy's spotless room, and a possible reason for it.

By the end of the visit she was much more cheerful because her Guider had pointed out that she had made a good start on five of the challenges without even knowing it.

Now that she was definitely on the way to becoming a Guide, Juliet was faced with several problems, one of them quite small, but urgent. She had been using Kate's Handbook, but Kate needed it back. The Handbook cost money and Juliet hated the thought of asking for it, because she knew every penny counted, and she didn't want her Guiding to seem like an extravagance.

She was musing on this one morning when she got to school. As she walked up the drive to it, several of the older pupils, mostly boys, swept by her on bicycles. Juliet was afraid they'd say something rude, either directly *to* her, or to one of their companions *about* her. To her surprise they did neither.

'Morning, young Juliet!' one of them called instead, quite cheerfully. All the same, after they'd hurried into school, Juliet slipped into the bicycle shed and spent some minutes there. She came out looking thoughtful.

The following weekend Juliet was painting a birthday card for Mum. One with butterflies on it. The result was not very good, but she knew her mother always liked a home-made card more than a shop one. The colours of the butterflies were not as bright as Juliet would have liked. 'Never mind,' she comforted herself. 'Next year's card will be much better because by then I'll have bought my new paints.' Then an idea came into her mind and she immediately wished it hadn't because it was the kind of idea that once you've had it, you can't get rid of.

A new paintbox and a pair of tights to give Mum would need all Juliet's saved-up pocket money. But if, having bought the tights, she didn't buy the paintbox, she could afford to buy the Guide Handbook for herself.

Then she took Kate's from the shelf and carefully copied from it the Guide Law, so that at least she'd always have that handy. When she reached the ninth law ('A Guide takes care of her own possessions and those of other people') she suddenly felt anxious about the book itself. She had put a brown paper jacket on it so it *should* be all right. Juliet knew better than to turn down the corner of pages or scribble in *any* book, but it would have been easy to put it down on something wet – for instance there was a greyish puddle of paint water on the desk *now*! She quickly mopped it up. There might have been grubby finger marks or accidentally bent pages, but she examined it carefully and all seemed well.

That evening, after a private meeting and their getting permission from all the right people concerned, the Kingfishers had decided to do something about the village square, as a Patrol. The little green patch near the Church had become neglected. People had thrown litter on it, and tramped across it. The little border round the edge was full of stones and weeds where there should have been flowers. Each member of the Patrol had bought something to help the project: trowels, forks, quite a lot of flowering plants just coming into bloom, (one of the patrol member's parents was a generous nursery-garden owner), seeds and edge-clippers. Juliet had been able only to produce herself and a lot of enthusiasm and energy. The others told her they were the most important items of all.

They were certainly needed. The stones were rough and the roots of the weeds — (funny, thought Juliet: they're called wild flowers when they grow where you want them to, and 'weeds' when they don't) had deep roots. Juliet's fingers were grazed and her nails broken, but there was also a great deal of laughing. When the others discovered that Juliet hated touching worms, they teased her dreadfully. Christine, the Patrol leader, pretended she'd put a worm down Juliet's neck. Juliet was so horrified as she protested and squealed and wriggled, feeling under her clothes to find the poor worm, that the others had to lean against each other to giggle better, until someone told her the truth.

'You beast!' exclaimed Juliet, and then was rather horrified to have spoken like that to her Patrol leader, but Christine didn't mind. Then Judy whispered to Juliet, 'She hates *leggy* creatures!' So presently Juliet said innocently to Christine. 'Oh *do* look at the interesting thing I've found!' and when Christine held out her hand, Juliet put into it an enormous beetle. Then it was Christine's turn to shriek, and what with one thing and another the job took longer than it might have. Passing people stopped to admire their work, and its results. The vicar came especially to say 'thank you', and several of the bigger boys from school said it wasn't a bad effort for girls, in spite of some boys from Belton who had gathered to jeer and whistle.

Finally Mrs Bailey appeared, and praised them and was told all the funny bits, which she enjoyed. There was a slight groan when she reminded them that all the tools must be cleaned and oiled before they were put away, but everyone agreed that the evening had been worth while. The square had never looked so pretty before.

Later, in bed, Juliet realised that she hadn't laughed so much since she'd come to the village.

5

Being Only Human

Next morning the pretty little village green had
become what Jimmie called 'a disaster area'. All
the bedding plants had been up-rooted and
thrown away to die. The bare patches of soil into
which seeds had been so carefully sown had been
scattered, the grass scarred by deep footprints,
and the carefully-trimmed edges of it were now
ragged and jagged.

The whole village was shocked and angry.
The news was passed between little groups of
people, across shop counters. The vicar asked
Mrs Bailey to pass on his condolences to the

Guides who had worked so hard. This she did, waiting for each Guide as they arrived at the school gates. 'The vicar says he was so grateful, and now he's very sorry. So am I. And of course I know just how *you* must feel. But please, *please* don't make matters worse by spreading rumours or gossip, or allowing your feelings to *show*. Remember the tenth Guide Law – "A Guide is self-controlled in all she thinks, says and does." '

The tenth law was easy to remember, but much more difficult to keep, especially when the school was buzzing and furious and sorry for the Kingfishers.

'Why? Why? Why?' everyone was asking, as were the grown-ups in the village. 'And *Who?*'

The big boys, led by Wayne, said they knew *who* well enough, and would soon put a stop to it. They were kind to the Kingfishers, and when someone said, with a look at Juliet, that nothing like this had happened before the *builders* had come to live there, Wayne actually told him to shut up and talk sense. Judy and Kate said this was kind of him. Juliet said nothing, keeping her thoughts to herself.

Three days later, Wayne didn't get to school until the morning break, and when he did, his arm was in a sling and everyone crowded round to hear what had happened. Juliet could see that he rather enjoyed talking about his injury but she didn't really blame him, anyone would, especially because it was rather an exciting, but horrid story.

He and Bill had been taking a stroll the previous evening, having a chat about what work they were going to be able to find themselves when they left school. At first they didn't notice that people seemed to be following them. Then they heard rustling in the bushes behind, and some whispering and began to wonder what was going on. Before they'd had time to wonder too much, they heard yells and shouting nearby.

'Nobody's voice we know,' said Bill. 'They wouldn't have played that kind of joke. If you can call it a joke.' He glanced at Wayne's sling, and everyone – or nearly everyone – could see his point. 'Then a bottle came whizzing through the air and hit Wayne on the arm.'

By now there was quite a crowd round the two boys. Judy and Kate and several of Juliet's new friends had become interested.

'I almost saw it in time,' Wayne said, 'but not quite. Of course I tried to bash it away. That's why it had to have eight stitches,' he added.

There were murmurs of sympathy and admiration. Eight stitches!

Juliet was sorry for Wayne and anyhow felt angry about anyone who threw things at people for fun. But again, in spite of being shy, she found herself asking in front of everybody. 'What did you do with the bottle?'

'We threw it into the ditch,' said Bill.

Juliet said, 'Pity, you should have kept it to show the Police. There might have been finger prints on it.' There were murmurs of agreement.

'You're quite right, young Juliet,' said Bill. 'We never thought of that. Stupid of us.'

Everyone looked at Juliet, and she felt hot all over.

'What did you do next?' several listeners wanted to know.

'Tried to ring the ambulance,' Bill said.

'I was bleeding rather badly,' Wayne put in, 'and I didn't want to upset the family. You know how they can be.'

'But we couldn't do it,' Bill went on, 'because some idiots had mucked up the telephone kiosk again.'

'Not *again*?' someone exclaimed.

'Yes, quite early,' said a girl. 'Auntie was taken poorly last night and our dad tried to ring from the phone-box, but the meter was smashed, and so was almost everything else.'

'It's disgusting!' said Wayne. 'We all know who's making the trouble. Something ought to be done about it.'

Next day Juliet tackled her bedroom properly. For some reason she couldn't explain to herself, she wanted to do it secretly. It was easy to fill cartons with absolute rubbish, such as smartie tubes, old magazines and tatty underclothes, and by moving the dressing-table and looking under her bed she found a number of peculiar things that had no reason to be saved. Also a lot of fluff. She soon filled three cartons. Then she took down some cups and cereal bowls which had no business to be there and quietly washed them up. In spite of some showers, she washed and dried most of her clothes, and then ironed what simply had to be ironed. She then did a little dusting and polishing and started vacuuming. Just as she was beginning to tell herself what a good daughter she was, and what a splendid Guide she would be, the vacuum cleaner picked up a paper-clip she hadn't noticed. The vacuum-cleaner (which Juliet thought should have been better designed; after all, everyone had paper-clips) got very agitated and noisy and finally produced some blue sparks and a hot-rubber smell, so she hurriedly switched it off and then had to own up to Dad that it had gone wrong while she was using it.

He wasn't at all pleased. After he had spent more than an hour taking the vacuum to pieces, and discovering the clip, and putting everything together again, he told Juliet she wasn't fit to touch any machinery and would she kindly not do so again.

'I was only turning out my room,' she protested.

'About time, I gather, from what your mother tells me.'

'It was about time,' said Juliet, 'that's why I was doing it.'

'I don't want any cheek from you,' said Dad, in his most growling voice.

Mum came into the room in time to hear this. 'What's going on?' she demanded.

Dad explained and Juliet explained, and unfortunately they both spoke very loudly and at the same time.

Mum tried to keep things peaceful. To Dad she said, 'She was doing her very best, Fred. Everyone has accidents. You know that. What about the bumper of your van that got bent against a tree?'

Dad looked even more annoyed and said, 'There's no need to go into all that now.'

Unwisely, Juliet – who hadn't known before about the bent bumper – said 'Why not? If we're going into all this about *my* accident, why can't we –?'

Mum interrupted sharply. 'Don't be rude to your dad, Juliet. You should have been more careful. He's got better things to do in the evenings than mend things you've broken. He's tired.'

'I'm tired too,' said Juliet. 'And I've got better things to do than make my room look absolutely spotless, which I've almost done, in case you hadn't noticed.'

She was horrified to hear the things her voice was saying all by itself.

'I *had* noticed, Juliet,' said Mum quickly. 'You've made a really good job of it. I'm very pleased. And I'm sure Mrs Bailey will be too, when I tell her.'

'What's it got to do with Mrs Bailey?' Dad demanded.

Juliet looked anxiously at Mum, who said, 'You know quite well that she's Juliet's Guider. The three of us have arranged that Juliet should keep her room in good order in future.'

She might perhaps have said more, but Dad said, 'Guides! I might have known they'd be at the bottom of this!'

Juliet thought that was a most unfair remark. So apparently did Mum, because she said, 'Now come along, Fred –'

But Dad wouldn't 'come along'. Instead he said, 'If this Guide palaver is going to make the child overtired and rude, she can pack it in. Remember what I said.'

Mum gave Juliet a look and said. 'Why don't you go out and get some fresh air while it's still light?'

Juliet went, feeling awful. She knew Mum and Dad were going to have yet another argument, and that it was all *her* fault again.

Jimmie and Steve were sitting on the garden wall, their heads close together.

'Go away!' said Jimmie as she got closer.

'I'm going,' said Juliet. 'I can't wait.'

This was evidently not the answer Jimmie had expected, or wanted. 'We're having a very secret discussion,' he said.

'You're welcome,' Juliet answered. 'I don't want to know anything about your secrets.'

'You would if you knew what they were about,' said Steve.

'You've been having a row,' Jimmie accused her. 'You've upset Dad again. How?'

'That's *my* secret,' said Juliet, and left them.

She decided to visit Judy. By now, she and Judy and Kate had all visited each other's houses and knew each others families, and Juliet had learned that being a Guide didn't necessarily mean you always behaved well. She knew several Guides who'd been quite the opposite, as well as her early surprised experience of Kate and Judy's conduct at school.

When she knocked at Judy's door it was answered by her mother who looked a bit fussed and said yes, of course she could see Judy, but that she was in the back garden with Kate. She didn't ask Juliet to go through the house, so she went through the little gate and found Judy and Kate in the summer house.

To her surprise, they both looked as gloomy

as she felt, though they were pleased to see her.

'Hello,' said Juliet cautiously, remembering Judy's mother's expression. 'Is anything wrong?'

'Yes,' said Kate and Judy at the same time.

Kate looked carefully at Juliet. 'Do you feel as awful as you look as if you feel?'

'After she'd worked this out, she said, 'Yes. Worse. If possible.'

'You'd better sit down then, because that makes three of us.'

She plumped down beside them. 'Tell me about it.'

'No, you first. We've been talking about our awfulnesses for quite some time. It would be a nice change to hear about somebody else's.'

It was very pleasant to have a sympathetic audience. Juliet told Kate and Judy all about what had happened at home, making things sound only a little worse than they actually had been, because her friends looked so miserable too.

When she'd finished the other two were suitably sorry for her.

'Now it's your turn,' she told them.

Kate said 'Most of my troubles have been my own fault, which only makes it worse. You're not in my maths set at school, or you'd know how badly I behaved this morning. I got everything wrong. Old "Gas-bag", that's Mr Gaston, who takes our set, said I was lazy, and could make much more effort if I really tried, and I said I couldn't and anyway I didn't want to. He said that was beside the point, and I said, "What point? The decimal-point?" '

'Kate!' Juliet was truly shocked. 'You didn't really *say* that?'

'I did!' admitted Kate wretchedly. 'I know it was terribly stupid and rude, but I get like that sometimes. I try and try and try not to, and then I sort of explode – you've heard me –'

Judy was nodding at Juliet. 'I told you she did.'

'Keep going, Kate,' Judy urged her, 'you'll feel better after you've told her everything.'

'I was trying to,' said Kate, 'but I can't if you keep interrupting –'

'*I* only interrupted once,' Juliet began, and realised she was interrupting again, so she snapped her mouth shut.

'– and of course old Gas-bag started to explode too – you know how gas *can* – and that made me worse until – Oh, well, he sent me to the Head and he gave me a fearful row and had a note sent round to Mum in the afternoon. Don't ask me who brought it – I expect he has spies everywhere. I guessed what had happened when Mum and Dad shut themselves in the sitting-room, and sure enough they asked me to go in, and said they were ashamed of me, and I was old enough to know better than to let them down like that, and what would happen when it came to important exams? Then *I* said I wouldn't bother to take them because I know I'd fail, and anyway what was the point in exams? I know loads of people who've passed them and still can't get a job, and Oh, never mind the rest! I thought the whole *house* would explode and right at the end, Mum said "What would your Guider say if she knew about this?" And that – that sort of finished me, and I dashed out and tore round here – and – and –'

Quite suddenly it was clear that her mother's remark had 'sort of finished her', so Judy and Juliet looked at each other and talked about nothing much until Kate had found her handkerchief and stopped using it.

Juliet felt terribly sorry for her, because she'd felt exactly the same way that very afternoon when she'd thought of Mrs Bailey knowing how she herself had behaved.

Then Judy said, 'I'm not the same as Kate. I don't actually explode, but I'm what Mum calls "scatty". I say I'll do things, and truly mean to, and then somehow I don't. Today I promised I'd bring home some gammon for tea, and I quite forgot about it. Mum got into a fuss and said there was hardly any time to catch the shop before it closed and probably all the fresh gammon would have been sold anyhow. I said I was sorry, and I'd rush back, but supposing the gammon had gone and what did she want instead? But *she* said it would be quicker to go herself and make up her own mind if necessary, than for me to go. She said "Keep an eye on Thomas, and on the washing because it looks as if it might rain again", and went. Thomas was quite happy in his playpen so I turned on the telly. Suddenly I heard the rain so I rushed out for the washing, but there was masses of it and the rain was heavy and some of the pegs would stick, you know the way they do, so most of the washing which had been nearly dry when I went out, got sopping. When I went indoors I found that wretched baby had somehow got out of his pen and done that thing people do in pantomimes, you know, pull the tablecloth from under the tea-things. If you're very quick, the trick works and all the china and stuff stays put, and it's clever. Sometimes it's *supposed* to go wrong and everything crashes down and then it's funny. Of course Thomas doesn't even know about the trick, so –'

'Oh *no*!' cried Juliet.

'Oh *yes*! There was a fearful mess and lots of things broken. Thomas was awfully pleased because the jam had landed right on him, so of course he was eating it with his hands –'

'Bet your Mum wasn't so pleased.'

Judy sighed. 'Well – you can imagine! There was the washing too, and she'd got caught in the rain without anything to put over her head and she'd had her hair done only yesterday.'

'Bet you another thing,' said Juliet. 'There wasn't any gammon.'

'Right, so sausages. But I didn't get any any-way. Mum said I didn't deserve tea, I'd better just keep out of sight. So I have, and I'm not looking forward to getting back into it again. I can tell you. I came into the summer-house because she told me not to sit on wet grass or I'd get rheumatism. I said I'd often sat on wet grass and hadn't got rheumatism yet. She'd said I'd be sorry when I was sixty and I said if things went on like this I'd never *get* to sixty –' Judy paused, suddenly appalled at herself – 'I can't quite re-member what else I said and I think I'd rather not try –'

Kate and Juliet were now looking appalled as well.

'We've certainly all made a real mess of today,' said Kate.

'It sounds unkind,' Juliet said, 'but in a way I'm glad to know that you too can get yourselves into trouble as well. I thought I was the only one.'

'Everyone does,' Kate said firmly, 'but we ought to be better than most, because we're . . .'

'Guides?' Juliet finished for her.

Judy said slowly, 'If you think, between us today we've broken nearly every law.'

'I'm not going to think like that,' said Juliet firmly. 'Being a Guide is terrific fun, but *nobody* can be expected to be perfect every minute. I'm sure all Guides must feel like that sometimes. After all, we *are* only human!'

6

Suspicions

For a time, after that disastrous day, things became a little quieter. Juliet and Kate and Judy did their best to keep out of every kind of trouble. Sometimes they succeeded. Sometimes they didn't. There were always the Guide meetings to look forward to and at half-term the whole Patrol (except for those whom families had made other arrangements) went on a picnic that lasted all day. The official reason for this was because they had volunteered to clean up a nearby copse, where more careless picnickers in the past had left litter of every kind, including plastic containers, rusty bits of bikes, and tin cans, which can hurt animals very much. In fact, although they took all the equipment to do this, and made a very good job of it, Juliet found that some Guides were using the opportunity to notice things to help them work for such badges as 'Backwoodsman' and 'Pioneer'. Mrs Bailey as well as organising the clearing of the rubbish, helped these Guides in every way she could.

'Everybody seems to be doing six things at once!' Juliet exclaimed.

'Everyone is,' Christine said. 'It's a habit you get into. I'm thinking of becoming a "Pioneer". You'll feel the same, once you're a proper Guide. Nothing you do is *ever* dull.'

Nothing was dull for unexpected reasons, too. Somehow the campfire wouldn't stay lit, and then there was the matter of some burnt potatoes, not to mention grazed knees, scorched fingers and two badly torn skirts, owing to a combination of carelessness and barbed wire. It was a pity that a sudden gust of wind blew up just as a large sackful of litter had overturned, which meant everybody chasing madly here and there to catch flying bits and pieces. But best of all was that everybody enjoyed every minute of it.

When Juliet got home she was exhausted, but scarlet with rushing about, and grinning to herself. She and Dad collided in the hall.

'Look where you're going, my girl!' said Dad.

Then he saw her face, and his own expression changed. 'Been with your precious Guides, have you?'

'Y-yes,' Juliet admitted.

Dad looked at the floor. 'Oh, well. As long as you like it. Don't mind me being a bit – well, things aren't always easy you know – I'm due for some good luck –'

Juliet knew what he was trying to say, and how difficult it was for him to say it. She suddenly hugged him. 'We *all* need good luck, Dad! Of course I understand.'

Dad went quickly upstairs.

Juliet always enjoyed her chats with Mrs Mitchell. During one of these, the old lady said 'Why don't you make a pressed flower album yourself?'

Juliet was not all that enthusiastic, but she pretended to be, out of politeness. So the following week she took Tramp on even longer walks and found lots of wild flowers she'd never come across before.

As Mrs Bailey had suggested, Mrs Mitchell had a book of flowers 'They call it "Conservation" now. Anything to use a long word – that's the way of things now-a-days. But it makes sense: it just means trying to keep safe the lovely old-fashioned plants which used to be everywhere, but are very few and precious now.'

So Juliet studied the pictures in the book carefully before she picked anything. It would have been very exciting if she had discovered a rare specimen, but she didn't, though she looked hard. She collected those which she knew were still common and put them carefully in a glass jar on the kitchen table so that she could take them to Mrs Mitchell who would make sure she had identified them properly. As she was going upstairs to change her shoes, she saw Dad go into the kitchen with a long roll of paper under his arm. When she came down again, he was sitting at the table studying a big map of the building site spread all over it.

Juliet asked. 'Where are my flowers?'

Dad, who didn't like being interrupted when he was working, kept his eyes on the plan and said irritably, 'What flowers?'

'They were in a jar on the table, just here.'

'Oh those,' said Dad. 'They weren't flowers, they were weeds.'

'They weren't weeds, they were wild flowers!' Juliet argued, beginning to feel hot with annoyance. Dad looked up. 'Look here, my girl, I don't claim to be an expert about the country, but even I know the difference between flowers and weeds.'

There was no point in arguing. So she said, 'Anyway, where are they?'

'In the dustbin where they belong,' said Dad. Juliet got hotter and hotter. Perhaps luckily, before she could say anything else, Mum came in from the back door. She looked from Dad to Juliet and said 'What's the trouble?'

'She's making another scene,' said Dad, 'just because I chucked out some weeds that were cluttering the place up.'

'They were some wild flowers I'd picked for Mrs Mitchell,' said Juliet.

Mum said, 'Oh dear. I did rather wonder when I saw them –' At that moment Juliet noticed with horror that her mother was carrying the kitchen bin and that it was empty. Mum had to move aside as Juliet rushed out past her and snatched off the lid of the big dustbin which was now nearly full of things like tin cans, and old wet cleaning rags, orange peel and dust from the vacuum and lots of tea-leaves. She knew at once that her precious flowers would be beyond saving, so she didn't try to find them.

In the kitchen Mum, who had obviously been having a quick word with Dad, gave Juliet a 'come with me' look, and went into the sitting-room. Juliet followed but she was so hot with fury that she knew exactly what Kate had meant when she said she 'exploded' and felt that she herself might do just that at any moment.

Mum understood and tried to be calming but Juliet found it very hard indeed to be calmed. One of the things she said was, 'He was wrong, and knew he was. But he didn't say "sorry" like

I'm supposed to when I've done something wrong.'

Mum said, 'You mustn't say things like that about Dad,' but Juliet said quite a lot of other things about him till at last Mum said, 'He's got so much on his mind at the moment, you must understand he's not his usual self and try to make allowances.'

'I've got a lot on my mind too,' said Juliet rebelliously, 'but he doesn't make allowances for *me.*'

'Listen, love. I know it's difficult for you to understand, but things are worse for him than you realise. There's been more vandalism on the site. The police know, and they think the less said the better at the moment, but your dad has to take a lot of responsibility. All this damage is causing hold-ups in the work, but the contract concerning it has a date for completion. And if the estate is *not* finished in time, there will be real problems and – can you keep a secret Juliet –?'

'A guide is loyal and can be trusted,' thought Juliet and said, 'Of course.'

Mum said quietly, 'It's possible that your dad could lose his job. At his age it wouldn't be easy for him to get another, and that would affect us all. So can you see how terribly worried he is?'

Juliet could. She had never realised that things were as bad as that. 'Someone had better find those vandals quickly,' she said. 'There are enough people looking for them. The proper Police, and a boy called Wayne Wilson at school has organised a sort of private police-force.'

'I don't have much faith in them,' said Mum, 'and the real Police are so short of men that they can't give as much time as they'd like to the problem. Even when the windows were smashed –'

'What windows?' asked Juliet.

'Oh dear, that's one of the things that we've been asked not to talk about. Still – now I've said that much, I might as well tell you the rest. A few weeks ago, somebody threw bricks through the office shed on the site and broke all the windows. There didn't seem to be much rhyme or reason. There was only a little petty cash inside. That was taken, but there was no need to have smashed all the windows.' Mum added anxiously. 'Now you won't repeat that will you, Juliet?'

Juliet was not keen to make a promise which she might find difficult to keep, so she said. 'Mum, can you remember exactly which day the windows were smashed?'

'It was in the night, as a matter of fact. A few days after all your lovely work on the village green was spoiled.'

Juliet did some rapid, private calculations. Then she called on Mrs Mitchell and took Tramp for another long walk. He was definitely in better shape now, and Juliet found enough wild flowers to replace the ones Dad had thrown away. When she took Tramp back to his owner, Mrs Mitchell was very pleased to see the new selection.

'Yes, you've learned all their names properly, and you haven't picked anything rare. Now you should start a collection of your own pressed wild flowers.'

Because she had to tell somebody, Juliet explained what had happened to her first little posy. Mrs Mitchell was sympathetic, but she didn't allow Juliet to feel sorry for herself or to be resentful.

'Your dad made a mistake,' she agreed. 'But we all make mistakes. Stop thinking about it. From what I hear he's been having more trouble at work.'

Mrs Mitchell, Juliet found, heard a good deal more than most people. Because her Mum had asked her not to talk about it, she felt she couldn't ask Mrs Mitchell for details. Instead she changed the subject to Guides, and presently was able to ask casually. 'Do you know our Guider?'

'Know her? Ann Henderson? Of course I do!' said Mrs Mitchell with a chuckle.

'Not Ann Henderson,' Juliet said anxiously. 'Mrs Bailey.'

'She might be Mrs Bailey to you – she's married now, of course. I'd almost forgotten, – but she's still Ann Henderson to me! I knew her

mother and grandmother. I knew Ann when she
was a baby squealing in her pram.'

Somehow the idea of Mrs Bailey, being a
squealing baby in a pram seemed funny, but
Juliet managed not to smile. Instead she asked.
'Then if she and her family have lived here all that
time, I suppose they'd know almost everybody?'

'Indeed they would,' said Mrs Mitchell.
'Why?'

'Well . . .' Juliet spoke carefully. 'I told you
that she managed to talk Dad into letting me join
the Guides, didn't I? I'm not quite sure how she
managed that, but Dad only let her in to the
house because instead of talking about Guides, at
first, she said she was sorry to hear about the
vandals on the building-site and perhaps she
could help. Do you think that was true, or just a
way of getting Dad to listen?'

'If Ann – if your Mrs Bailey – said that, then
she was speaking the truth. She'd never tell a lie,
that one.'

'That's what I thought,' said Juliet. 'So she
might know – or think she knows – who's
doing these things?'

'If she does, then she'll do her best to put
matters right, never worry. Anyhow, there's
nothing *you* can do about it.'

'There might be,' Juliet said slowly, knowing
the old lady's sharp eyes were on her. 'I've got
my suspicions too.'

'Then keep them to yourself, young lady,' said Mrs Mitchell sharply. 'Don't go interfering in what's not your concern.'

'It *is* my concern, because of Dad,' said Juliet.

'Ah,' said Mrs Mitchell, 'but you're too young to be meddling with things of this kind. Leave them to older folk who know better. I expect you've been putting two and two together and making five, and all based on gossip, at that.'

'No.' This time Juliet was firm. 'Not based on gossip. Based on things I've noticed for myself.'

'You've got an imagination, my girl,' said Mrs Mitchell reprovingly, as though an imagination was a bad thing to have, like spots, or whooping-cough. 'Just see that it doesn't run away with you. My father used to say, "Imagination is a good servant, but a bad master". Remember that. Anyhow, I don't expect you have much time to imagine things. You must be very busy keeping up with your school work, and learning to be a Guide. How is it all going?'

'School's better. They still make you do about a million times more homework than they ought to –'

Mrs Mitchell laughed again. 'I wonder if there's ever been a child who hasn't said that!'

'It's true all the same,' said Juliet defensively. 'Otherwise it's not too bad. And I know quite a lot of people now. Guiding is great though, and there's an awful lot to learn –'

'A good thing,' said Mrs Mitchell, who was now placidly knitting. 'Satan finds work for idle hands.'

'Did your father used to say that too?' Juliet asked rather naughtily.

Mrs Mitchell gave her a sharp look. 'That's enough, young lady. Tell me more. What kind of things do you have to learn?'

Juliet recited the Guide law.

'Hmm,' said Mrs Mitchell at the end. 'You'd have to be a saint to keep that law all the time. So you can only *try* to keep it.'

'Yes, that's what Mrs Bailey said,' said Juliet. She added, 'I'm afraid I've got to go now. It's Mum's birthday tomorrow and I must wrap her present. Not that it will be very difficult,' she admitted, 'because it's only a pair of tights.'

'Have you remembered a card?'

Juliet was glad to have been asked, so that she could say 'Of course. I always paint her one myself. She likes that.'

Mrs Mitchell nodded. 'Yes. She would.'

Juliet wondered whether to tell the old lady, who knew she'd been saving up for paints, of her decision to buy the Handbook. It might sound a bit like boasting, but it would be rather nice to know that *somebody* knew of her unselfish decision, and say 'Well done'. So she did tell Mrs Mitchell, who *didn't* say, 'Well done'. She only said 'You couldn't do anything else, could you?'

Which made Juliet, who had been hoping to be praised, feel rather flat, till Mrs Mitchell added. 'You told me you were planning to spend your savings on paints, but I was so certain that you'd think it for yourself that – go and take that parcel from the sideboard drawer.' Juliet did, and went to hand it to Mrs Mitchell who snapped, 'Don't give it to *me*. It's got a name on, hasn't it?'

Juliet saw that it had: her own. 'A present?' she asked, surprised. 'It's not my birthday or anything.'

'Who said anything about birthdays? There are lots of days between birthdays. Why waste them?'

Juliet thought that was a very sensible line to take, especially as the present was heavy and interesting to feel. She opened it at once. There were two things inside. One was an empty album.

'That's for your flower collection,' said Mrs Mitchell. Juliet realised she would *have* to use it now.

The other thing was a truly beautiful paint-box. Juliet said 'It must have been terribly expensive,' but stopped herself, because she realised just in time that it might sound rude. She wanted suddenly to kiss Mrs Mitchell, but she looked rather unkissable. So Juliet just stood staring at the paintbox, finding it difficult to say anything else.

Mrs Mitchell was very matter-of-fact. 'I'm glad you're pleased. Look after it. By the way, I had a talk with your mother the other day. A very wise and kind person.'

'Was it about me?' Juliet asked nervously.

'Why should you think we had nothing better to talk about than you?' said Mrs Mitchell crisply. 'There's a bit of washing up to do, then you'd better be off.'

On her way home Juliet wondered why she was becoming so fond of Mrs Mitchell and decided it was because the old lady said exactly what she thought, even if it wasn't what her listener hoped she'd say. Also, she seemed to know a great deal about people, and how difficult life could be for everyone; not just lonely people of her own age, but young ones too. Well, she ought to, having lived so long.

7

Birthday, and an Adventure

Mum's birthday came, and everything went off
very well. She was pleased with the card, and
said the tights were just what she needed and so
was the cardigan Dad gave her, and the book that
Jimmie produced. It was a history of cars, and
Juliet had her own thoughts about it because
Jimmie was interested in cars, and Mum wasn't.
She watched Mum looking pleased about the
present, and remembered Mrs Mitchell saying
she was a 'wise and kind person', and decided
that, as usual, Mrs Mitchell had been right.

There was a birthday cake too. Juliet had tried

to make it secretly herself at the weekend while Mum was out shopping, and Dad was 'having a quick look at the paper', which actually meant having a little nap in the sitting room with the newspaper over his face. Unfortunately Jimmie and Steve had discovered what she was doing, and insisted on trying to help, which annoyed her, though at first she tried not to show it.

By reading Mum's cookery book she made a mixture which was supposed to end up as a light and fluffy sponge-cake. Jimmie would keep on opening the oven to see how the cake was doing (although the book said you shouldn't because letting the cold air in would stop the cake rising). At last Juliet could bear it no longer and forgot about the tenth Guide Law saying she should be 'self-controlled in all she thinks and says and does', and was not controlled at all. She told Jimmie he was an interfering nuisance and he called her a Bossyboots.

The book had been right though, because as a result of what he had done, the two halves of the cake ended up by looking more like two tough pancakes. To make things worse, both boys insisted on helping to make butter-icing to go in the middle, and a different kind of icing for the top, the part that Juliet had been looking forward to most. They then ran off, leaving her to do the washing-up. She had to be quick, because of Mum coming home at any minute. She more or less managed, though she didn't do as good a job on the cooker as she'd meant to. Mum didn't seem to notice anything. When the actual birthday happened, it was one of those lovely warm days, so it all turned into a family picnic with Steve coming along too. ('Must taste *our* cake!') Dad was either in a much better mood than usual, or was at least pretending to be. Mum wore the blue cardigan Dad had given her, and Dad seemed almost his old self, even whispering 'Well done, my Julietta' when he heard she'd made the cake. When the time came to cut it, everyone bravely had some and said it was delicious, although it wasn't. At one point, Jimmie – very meanly, because it was his fault – started to make a joke about the icing and cement. Juliet gave him a black look and he stopped, realising that talking about cement might lead to talking about cement-mixers, which, with Dad there, would not have been at all suitable, especially when Dad was doing his best to join in.

A week later, on a showery day, Juliet ran into Jimmie and Steve during her walk with Tramp, and they decided to explore a nearby hill together. They scrambled upwards, while Tramp ran yelping happily beside them. Juliet was slightly slower because she was noticing things which might help them if they got lost coming back. So she took good care to remember a telephone kiosk, an old large lichen-covered stone, the shape of a young sycamore tree bent by the wind, a narrow road crossing their track, and similar landmarks. She knew that, as a Guide, she ought to have a compass with her and know how to use it, but she hadn't got one, and wouldn't have understood it if she had, so she did the best that she could without it.

It was as well that she did, because of what happened next. They came to a broad stream tumbling downwards over water-smoothed stones, and Jimmie said, 'No problem. We can easily leap over *that*.' Tramp had already done so. Juliet saw Jimmie wink at Steve, and knew why. She was not a leaping sort of person, and her brother teasingly wanted to prove it. She looked anxiously at the stream. She would *have* to do it, somehow.

Jimmie jumped first. He cleared the water easily. Juliet thought she'd better follow quickly, before she got too frightened. As if it were no trouble at all, she made a tremendous effort and landed safely beside Jimmie.

It was Steve who got it wrong. He ended up half in and half out of the water, and instead of scrambling out, he stayed where he was, and his face turned a strange greenish colour.

'Come on!' shouted Jimmie.

'I can't,' said Steve with a gasp, and Juliet saw immediately that he couldn't. One leg still dangled in the water, probably because his foot had struck a stone hidden by ripples. She also saw that when Steve did his best to haul himself on to the bank, one of his arms looked twisted and peculiar, and was obviously no use to him. Jimmie could only stare horrified, but Juliet's mind began to work. Desperately she tried to remember all that she had heard about first aid at her very first Guide meeting. She guessed that Steve was in a state of 'shock', and knew that he should be calmed and gently put into the 'recovery position', so she quickly said, 'It's all right, Steve, we can cope.'

Jimmie was not coping at all, so Juliet said, 'Don't stand there gawping. Help me very carefully to lift him out of the water. If we joggle him, we might make things worse.'

They did this, though Jimmie's face was getting rather like Steve's to look at.

'Leave him a moment,' ordered Juliet. 'Steve, where's it hurting most?'

'My arm,' said Steve faintly. 'And my ankle.'

'Loosen tight clothing – wrap in a blanket but do not over-heat,' Juliet remembered Mrs Bailey saying. None of Steve's clothes were tight, there was no blanket to hand, or any chance of over-heating on the chill, damp hillside.

'Do not give anything to eat or drink' had been another instruction. No problem, because they had nothing to eat or drink with them. She knew

Steve ought to go to the casualty department of a hospital at once. Difficult, but it had to be done. 'We must get him to a hospital,' she told Jimmie and showed him how they could grasp each others' wrists to make a chair for Steve. 'But first I think we ought to support his arm and his ankle,' she said, rather panicky because she was not absolutely sure if she was doing the right things. But Steve's arm looked as if it were in the correct position already for a sling. Because of the clouds, Juliet had brought a headsquare, and this made a very good one, and she actually remembered, having practised on Judy, a 'pretend patient', how to make it work. Poor Steve made little moaning noises while she did it, but she pretended not to hear them. Jimmie produced a large and rather dirty handkerchief and Juliet, a little less panicky now, used it as a bandage for Steve's ankle.

'Now,' she said firmly to her brother. 'Hold on tight and off we go.'

Of course the most difficult part was re-crossing the stream. 'We'll just have to wade through and get our shoes sopping,' said Juliet.

'But what'll Mum say, and Dad?' asked Jimmie in horror.

'I don't know, and I don't care at the moment,' said Juliet in the kind of voice that made Jimmie obey her at once.

Steve said nothing at all, though he could not

help gasping and crying out which worried Juliet, but there didn't seem to be much she could do about it. Instead she concentrated on re-tracing their path exactly by means of the land-marks she had noticed. When Jimmie twice con-tradicted her, she was able to squash him very easily. Steve seemed to get heavier and heavier and their wrists ached. Juliet began to feel rather desperate.

Then Jimmie said, 'Look, a cottage over there. We could telephone.'

Juliet looked, and said, 'We can't.'

'Why not?' Jimmie demanded, tired of being useless.

'Because they haven't got a telephone, no wires,' said Juliet briefly. 'We could go in and rest but I think it's more important to get an ambulance, so we'll phone from the public box at the bottom of this hill down this lane. It's much closer, anyhow.'

Jimmie said, 'We can't use it! We haven't any money!'

Juliet said, '*I* have. Guides always carry enough to telephone if necessary. But an emergency-call costs nothing, in case you didn't know.'

They then concentrated on putting Steve as gently as possible on the ground. 'Stay with him,' Juliet commanded her brother. She then ran down to the kiosk. For a wonder, it was in order. She made the call for an ambulance, not forgetting to say exactly where they were. It arrived very soon. Juliet explained what had happened to the two kind men in it. They at once produced a stretcher, and made jokes to Steve, who tried to make some of his own. Jimmie went to hospital in the ambulance to keep Steve company, while Juliet with Tramp, yelping and puzzled by all that had happened, raced back to the village to tell Steve's parents the whole story.

It was only after she had done all this that her legs began to feel shaky.

Next day Juliet was a heroine, and she hated it. The news of Steve's accident and how she had handled it, flew round the village. His parents called on Juliet to thank her for all she'd done for him. It appeared that his ankle had only been sprained but that his arm had been broken. 'What would have happened if your Juliet hadn't been there?' Steve's mother asked Mum.

'I couldn't have managed without Jimmie,' Juliet said truthfully. 'It needed two of us.'

'Ah, but it was you who took charge and knew what to do.'

After the visit Mum couldn't stop being pleased and proud. Juliet, glad to be able to make it clear in front of Dad, said, 'I couldn't have taken charge and known what to do, if I hadn't been a Guide.'

Mum looked at Dad and said, 'There now. See what the Guides have taught her?'

But Dad said. 'Guides? Nothing! I've always known she's got some commonsense if only she'd use it.'

Juliet and Mum knew he was only being stubborn, so they glanced at each other but said nothing.

Mrs Mitchell was a great comfort. Of course she knew all about everything, as usual, but she didn't go on and on about it. She just said, 'A good thing you didn't lose your head like you usually do. Poor little Steve, that arm will keep him off cricket for weeks, I'm afraid.'

Mrs Bailey said some extremely pleasant things about Juliet at the next Guide meeting, and pointed out how valuable it was that she had listened carefully at her very first Company meeting, although not yet a Guide, so that when the emergency came Juliet had 'Been Prepared'.

Juliet was just beginning to go red because of course everyone stared at her, when Mrs Bailey suddenly changed the subject to another which interested everyone. It was only a few weeks to the end of the school term, she reminded them, and therefore the end of the regular Guide meetings. The last of the summer was usually a celebration of some kind, and she asked the Company if anyone in it had any particular thoughts about how this might be done.

Nobody produced any very original ideas, so at last Mrs Bailey said. 'I was wondering if you would like to hold a barbecue in my garden?'

Everybody was so enthusiastic about this that she said quickly, 'There will be difficulties, of course. First, we shall hope for fine weather. I'm very lucky to have a large garage, so that we could move into that, if necessary, but it would be far more exciting to hold it out of doors. Secondly I wondered if it would be a good idea to ask all your families? If so, there would have to be a good deal of food, and I would have to ask you and your parents to help provide some of it. Thirdly, there will have to be a number of you to plan the menus, and to help cook it on the night, and help me to look after all the visitors. Those of you planning to take your Hostess Badge will probably be interested in that part, because it will help you to win it.'

An excited buzz broke out, because now everyone was having different ideas at the same time. After a little while, Mrs Bailey stopped the noise to say in a serious voice. 'I see that you think it's a good idea. But it will mean not only a great deal of hard work but discussions with your parents first to see how they feel. If they are pleased to join in, I suggest that each Patrol leader discusses with her Patrol how they can best help, and then that the Patrol leaders have a meeting between themselves to see how all the plans fit together. After that I can have a chat with the Patrol leaders to tie up any loose ends.'

By this time nobody was talking about Juliet any more, and she was extremely glad, though she did privately wonder what Dad would say when he was invited to a Guide barbecue. She could imagine all too well his face when he even heard of it, so she tried to put it out of her mind.

This was made easier later, because Jimmie and Steve put something quite different into it. Jimmie said. 'Because of what you did, we're going to let you in on our secret.'

'I don't want to be,' said Juliet.

'Then you ought, when you know what it's about. It's the vandals and the way they're messing up Dad's site.' After that Juliet did listen.

'We're determined to find out who's got it in for him, so we're a secret detective agency.'

'Goodness!' said Juliet. 'Who isn't? The proper police are detecting, and then there's Wayne and Bill —'

'They're not all that good,' said Steve.

'How do you know?' Juliet asked.

'If we tell you, will you promise not to let on?' said Jimmie.

'I'll see,' said Juliet. She was so certain that both Jimmie and Steve *wanted* to tell her their information that she suspected she could get away without promising, and she was right.

'The thing *is*,' Steve said, 'they're not as well

organised as they ought to be. Everybody knows that Wayne and Bill tell the others where they've got to be, and at what times. The point is, that some of them aren't at the right places at the right times.'

'We did some secret checking up,' Jimmie admitted, 'and there the right people weren't, if you know what I mean.'

'Not only the lazy ones who'd you expect to skive off, either,' said Steve. 'Once it was Bill. He doesn't know that we know, so mind you don't let on. You promised.'

'I didn't,' said Juliet quickly. 'You just thought I was going to.'

'Of all the –!' Jimmie exclaimed with fury.

'Never mind,' said Juliet impatiently. 'I won't tell anyone. Not now, anyway. Now I've got to be off because I'm going to see Mrs Bailey.'

That was true. Her Guider had asked her to call in for a few words. Juliet wondered what they could be. She was astonished when she found what they were.

Mrs Bailey said, 'I thought it was time we had another look at the eight challenges, Juliet.' So they did.

'Last time we discussed the challenges,' Mrs Bailey said, 'you were doing well in all but three. "Homemaker", "Thinking for Yourself" and "Exploring the Arts". Since then you've begun your pressed flower album, Mrs Mitchell tells me, so that can count as a new way of Exploring the Arts. You certainly thought for Yourself when poor Steve had his accident, didn't you? And your mother has signed the form to say that your bedroom has been very different from what it was, and you've tried to be more helpful and tidy generally.'

'She never told me!' Juliet exclaimed.

'No,' Mrs Bailey was smiling. 'I asked her not to. Now, if we count up, we'll find that you have succeeded in all of the eight challenges. So that means you are qualified to join the Company. *I* think you're ready. Do you?'

For a moment Juliet stood with her mouth open and her mind a blank. Then it began to think again, and she said 'Honestly – *no*.'

'Good,' said Mrs Bailey surprisingly. 'Just the answer I was hoping for. That means you realise you've got a long, long way to go, like every other Guide. If you'd said "Yes", I'm sure ready' then *I* wouldn't have been sure that you were! Now are you absolutely certain that you *want* to become a Guide?'

This time, Juliet didn't need to think at all. 'Oh yes!' she said.

'Then we must make sure that you understand the Guide Promise, and how to make it.'

Mrs Bailey was now very serious, and Juliet felt serious too. They spent a quiet half-hour together, at the end of which Juliet realised how very important the Guide Promise was. Then Mrs Bailey said, 'There are only the details to sort out. We're always glad to welcome a new Guide into the Company, and if possible to make a ceremony out of it. As we're going to have a barbecue soon, that would seem to be the ideal occasion for you to join.'

Juliet knew she would be the only new Guide to make the promise. She realised that all the families were to be invited. She imagined how it would feel to have to make the Promise with everybody looking and listening.

'I couldn't do it,' she quavered.

'Nonsense.' Mrs Bailey was exceedingly brisk. 'If you're ready to make the Promise – and I think you are – then you certainly won't make your own self-consciousness a reason to prevent it. You must realise, Juliet, about which things are the most important.'

Although her Guider was right, and Juliet knew it, she still had a very trembly feeling inside, and she thought the best thing to do would be to remove herself before it showed more on the outside. So she did.

At home, she found a quiet moment in which to tell Mum that Mrs Bailey thought she was ready to become a proper Guide. Mum gave her a great big hug, and another when she heard that it was all to happen at the barbecue. She said, 'Well done, love. I always knew you'd make it.

Don't worry about other people being there. I know just how you must feel about *that*, but *I'll* be there, anyhow, and I've put enough by to do my share of providing food. I'm very proud of you, love, so don't forget it.'

Juliet suddenly found it necessary to go to her bedroom and do something about her face. When she came downstairs again, she found that Dad, Jimmie and Steve were there and had been discussing the Guide Barbecue and that she was to make the Promise there.

Jimmie said: 'I'll come. A free Barbecue. Great!'

Steve said, 'I'll be there too. After all, I'm as good as one of the family now!'

Dad said: 'More Guide nonsense. Waste of time and money. Count me out.'

Juliet would have had more time to worry about that, had not something very startling happened almost at once.

8

'So Much to Do . . .'

Early next morning, Dad had a call from the police. Somebody had set fire to his shed on site and the blaze was already well away before a neighbour had seen and reported it. The fire engine had been called and saved as much as they could. The police were there now, and wanting to see Dad at once, and anyone who might be able to help.

Juliet, on hearing this, threw on her clothes without even bothering to wash, do her hair, or clean her teeth, and rushed through the kitchen, where Mum, though terribly worried, was poaching eggs. She cried, 'Where are you going? You haven't had breakfast – your satchel's in the living-room –' But Juliet only yelled, 'Sorry, Mum! Must rush! Now!' And rushed. Naturally to Dad's site.

Because she was in an even more noticing mood than usual, in spite of her haste, Juliet even saw something small, half-buried in the grass, and because it was not grass-coloured, she paused briefly to pick it up, look at it carefully, and put it in her pocket, before joining everyone else.

People gazed with interest at the charred shed, and chattered amongst themselves about who ever could have done it.

Wayne and Bill were both talking the loudest of all about how disgraceful it was – obviously the work of the Belton boys, and that they'd catch them yet.

Rather disappointingly, the fire-engine had gone, but Sergeant Morgan the local policeman was there, and a great many other people, amongst them people from school, including Wayne and Bill, some of their gang, Steve and Jimmie, and, rather surprisingly, Mrs Bailey.

Suddenly Sergeant Morgan became very strict and started to order people about. Apparently an Inspector was on his way and he would not be pleased to find the area crowded and trampled. Posts and wires were hastily fixed around the shed, some distance from it, and it was obvious that no work would be done on the site that day. Juliet saw Dad's face when this was announced and she quite forgot their recent squabbles and upsets and only remembered that they were really very fond of each other, and knew that she couldn't bear him to look so worried and angry and sad and that she must do everything she could to help. She had read many books, and seen many television plays in which the Baddies had been caught by a certain trick. Of course she knew that real life was usually very different from stories and plays, but the trick might work and therefore was worth a try.

So when Sergeant Morgan said loudly and firmly through a megaphone: 'I would be obliged if, unless anybody has any information, you would all kindly leave so that we can proceed with our investigations –' she found herself once again seized by the quite extraordinary urge to speak out that she'd had before, and suddenly piped up, 'I've got some information!'

Although she was so frightened that her voice was only a terrified squeak, it was heard, every single face in the crowd turned towards her, and silence fell. It was exactly like the very worst kind of nightmare she had ever had and she wished she could sink straight into the muddy ground.

As it was, she *had* to go on. Because she was

not absolutely sure that what she was going to say was the truth, she crossed her fingers behind her back, though she was uneasily aware that the Guide Law made no mention of the crossing of fingers for this reason. She also had the horrible fear that if she publicly accused the wrong people it would be wicked and cruel. So it was a very, very nervous Juliet who said: 'I think I know who's been doing all these things.'

There was a gasp from everyone, which didn't help.

Sergeant Morgan said grimly, 'Would you like to speak to me privately?' But Juliet *had* to say. 'No, I'd rather speak now,' partly because if she didn't get her nightmare finished quickly she wouldn't be able to bear it, and partly because if she spoke privately there would be no hope of her trick working.

She was feeling so dreadful by now that the watching listening people had almost faded in to a blur as she said loudly and clearly. 'I'd much rather that Wayne and Bill told you about it than me.'

Everybody looked at Wayne and Bill both of whose mouths were hanging open. Sergeant Morgan said to them, 'Can you help us?' but they shook their heads in an amazed way Wayne said, 'How could we? We didn't know anything about the fire till we saw the crowd.'

So Juliet had to go on, though carefully. She

said: 'I'd hoped they could have explained some
things I know about. Wayne and Bill and some
others didn't want a housing estate here, and
they'd got it in for my dad and for me. At first
they said so, and then they suddenly started to be
nice. I'm afraid that made me suspicious. I didn't
say anything to anyone, but I did begin to wonder a bit, especially when, every time things
happened, they blamed the Belton boys. Wayne
even got his gang to be detectives, but I think he
did that just to make people think that *he* had
nothing to do with any trouble.'

'Here, hang on!' cried Wayne furiously.

The Sergeant held up his hand. 'A moment
please. I think we ought to let the young lady
finish.'

Everyone else was silent now. It was awful,
but Juliet struggled bravely on. 'I'm dreadfully
dreadfully, sorry if I'm wrong, but it did all seem
rather odd. I *know* that Wayne made lists of
where his spies were supposed to be at certain
times, but those people were not always in those
places at those times, and none of them quite
knew who was where or when. So it was easy for
Wayne to be somewhere else doing something
that –'

'Make her shut up!' Wayne roared at Sergeant
Morgan. But he only held up his hand again and
nodded at Juliet.

Her mouth was so dry she could hardly speak.

'There were other things. Somebody wrote a nasty message in green paint on the cement mixer. Later I found the very same colour paint marks on Wayne's bicycle saddle; not on top, where it looked as if something might have been scrubbed off, but underneath, where it didn't show.'

Of course everyone looked at Wayne, but he only glared back.

'Another funny thing was that he had a cut arm just after the shed windows had been broken. I worked it out. Wayne told us how it was supposed to have happened, and that only Bill was with him, but *Bill* said –' Juliet stopped abruptly and on purpose, terribly afraid.

'I told everyone about the bottle being thrown,' put in Bill very quickly.

Juliet faced him directly, though her heart was secretly bumping. 'Are you absolutely *sure* that you told everybody the same story?'

Then she held her breath, because if things didn't go exactly as she'd hoped they would, and at this very moment, she'd know her trick had failed.

But Wayne had already turned furiously on Bill. 'You better had be! You *swore* you would!' Then he suddenly realised what he'd said, and stopped, but not before Bill had shouted, 'I did! I did! I never said a word about how it really –' Then he stopped too. 'I don't know what she's on about,' he finished, feebly.

There was a buzz from the crowd which Sergeant Morgan quickly stopped. Juliet was less afraid now, because she was more sure she'd been right all along. In order to make certain, she said to Wayne. 'But you must admit that you've been on this site before?'

'Certainly not!' exploded Wayne. 'It's private property. Everyone knows that. I've never been near it till a few moments ago.'

'But,' said Juliet with the last of her courage, 'I came in by the opposite gate from you. So if you've never been here before, how is it that I've just found *this* on the other side of the site?' She held out her hand. In it was the small object that she had picked out of the grass: a bright blue match-holder with Wayne's own initials on it, W. W. in gold, exactly like the one with which he had, so many weeks ago, tried to impress his friends at school. A good many of them were in the crowd this morning.

Wayne had gone white. 'I gave it to Bill,' he said.

Bill snarled, 'You rotten liar! You never did! I know why they're here as well as you do!' Juliet, feeling very trembly, handed the matches to Sergeant Morgan, who looked from them to the half-burned shed and then to Wayne. But by that time Wayne and Bill were fighting and calling each other dreadful names.

After that a lot of things happened at once. Mum suddenly appeared and took Juliet home. Juliet knew her trick had worked and that she'd discovered the vandals, but felt mean about it in a strange way, and she was not very well for several days, even though she tried to be. During that time there was a lot of talk, and the talkers included Mum, Dad, Mrs Bailey, Wayne, Bill, some of their friends, Mrs Mitchell and the Police. Mrs Mitchell and Mrs Bailey seemed mysteriously to know quite a lot about how telephone kiosks had been damaged, plants up-rooted and tyres slashed. Everything was horrible.

Suddenly it was the day of the Barbecue.

Juliet was determined to be there, and she was. She was sorry to have had to miss helping with the preparations, but Mrs Bailey visited her, and though she said little, she made it clear that Juliet in spite of this and that – had acted as a Guide should, and that now that the rumpus of the vandals was over, she should think only of herself for the moment. Juliet had said she felt very sorry about Wayne, but Mrs Bailey said, 'Don't be. Poor Wayne has been needing help for some time, and now he will get it. You've no need to feel guilty.'

Just before the Barbecue began, Juliet, in second-hand uniform, whispered to Mum, 'I don't think I can go through with it. Honestly.

All those people, and – and –'

'Nonsense, Love,' Mum said very firmly indeed. 'You can't let us all down now. And think of that lovely supper afterwards!'

'Oh *no*!' wailed Juliet. 'Don't talk about food! I feel sick if I even think of it! I can't possible eat a *thing*!'

She couldn't either. Even a cup of tea or a dry biscuit. But she did see that she had to do her best, so – somehow – she found herself in Mrs Bailey's garden, which had been transformed by the Company. The barbecue glowed, coloured lanterns hung amongst the trees, and brilliant fairy-lights looped between them, with a background of darkening skies already pricked with stars. The air was warm and scented, and the garden full of people whose faces were lit with happiness and excitement.

As the Company meeting began formally, voices were hushed. Then the moment came when Juliet found herself, for a few minutes, the most important person amongst the blurred, pale faces round her. But she knew Mum was amongst the watchers, also Jimmie and Steve. Of course Kate and Judy were there anyway. Lastly, to her surprise, she spotted Mrs Mitchell with Tramp on a very short lead because he was interested in the barbecue smells.

Then there was silence and lights and somehow she found herself standing before Mrs

Bailey, her Guider who was asking:—

'Do you understand that as a Guide you will be trusted to do your best: to do your duty to God, to serve the Queen, and help other people, and to keep the Guide Law?'

Juliet said. 'Yes.'

Her Guider then asked: 'Are you willing to make your Promise as a Guide?'

Juliet said, 'Yes. I promise I will do my best:

To do my duty to God, to serve the Queen and help other people, and to keep the Guide Law.'

Her Guider said: 'I trust you to keep this Promise, and to try to do at least one Good Turn every day.'

Mrs Bailey then pinned the Guide Badge on to Juliet's tie, and said in a very few words, how she and everyone present were very pleased that now she was one of the world family of Guides.

Juliet was relieved that she had been able to make her replies loudly and clearly, but still her eyes felt hot.

Mrs Bailey smiled very kindly, making Juliet blink, which seemed stupid really, because all her Company and her friends were clapping and smiling.

Then suddenly, looking towards her own family, she was astonished to see Dad — yes *Dad*! sitting beside Mum and clapping as hard as anyone, and Juliet suspected, feeling a bit blinkish himself.

A tear escaped and trickled slowly down the side of her nose because two very happy things were happening at once, becoming a Guide, and knowing that she and Dad were friends again.

She quickly wiped away the tear and suddenly everyone was round her and smiling and laughing, and it was time to start eating.

And oh, she was so hungry!

More Beaver Books

On the following pages you will find some other exciting Beaver Books to look out for in your local bookshop

THE FILE ON FRAULEIN BERG

Joan Lingard

Sally, Harriet and Kate are very suspicious of Fraulein Berg. She appears to have a somewhat mysterious past and they can't really understand what a German teacher is doing in Belfast in 1944.

They decide to keep 'tabs' on her and they open a file on Fraulein Berg – recording her movements, her friends and anything they can discover about her.

The consequences of their detective work are dramatic and far reaching, and completely unexpected!

THE SIEGE OF THE WHITE DEER PARK

Colin Dann

The peace of White Deer Park nature reserve is threatened by a mysterious predator, so silent, so stealthy, so cunning and efficient that it kills again and again – undetected.

Animals from outside pour into the nature reserve, desperately seeking safety from the killer, but in vain. It is as though the park is under siege. Fox and his companions are resourceful and they have come through many crises before. Can they track down the killer and rout him from the park before it is too late?

This is the fifth exciting title in the award winning Farthing Wood series.

JESS AND THE RIVER KIDS

Judith O'Neill

Jess loved the river. She liked to go there for peaceful Sunday afternoons, painting or reading. But one day she arrived to find two boys already on her stretch. Surely they had no right to be there – it was her place!

Gradually Jess became friends with Kenny and Snowy. She liked the houseboat they lived on – and old Lizzie who was looking after them while their Dad was at war and their Mum away. But the pattern of their tranquil summer days was disturbed when a fire broke out on the boat. How did it start? And why was one cabin turned completely upside down?

A prizewinning book at the Adelaide Festival of Arts.

BUT JASPER CAME INSTEAD

Christine Nostlinger

It was Tom who was supposed to go and stay with the family in Vienna. But Jasper went instead. And, as thirteen-year-old Ewald and his sister Billie were soon to find out, Jasper was quite a handful. He didn't like washing, for a start. Or the food. And he certainly didn't want to go on outings.

How the family deal with disaster on disaster makes for a hilarious – and moving – story.

YOU TWO

Jean Ure

Elizabeth's world had crashed around her. Her Dad had lost his job and the family were moving to a smaller house. Even worse, it seemed she would have to leave the select private school she loved to go to a large comprehensive.

Gladeside was about a million miles away from Lady Margaret's. No uniform, huge classes and noisy, rude children who made fun of her 'posh' accent. Elizabeth was sure she wouldn't fit in. But then she hadn't met Paddy Dewer and become half of a very special partnership called 'You-Two'.

A true-to-life school story for girls of around nine to eleven.

If you're an eager Beaver reader, perhaps you ought to try some more of our exciting titles. They are available in bookshops or they can be ordered directly from us. Just complete the form below and enclose the right amount of money and the books will be sent to you at home.

☐	THE SUMMER OF THE WAREHOUSE	Sally Bicknell	£1.25
☐	THE GOOSEBERRY	Joan Lingard	£1.25
☐	FOX CUB BOLD	Colin Dann	£1.50
☐	GHOSTLY AND GHASTLY	Barbara Ireson Ed.	£1.50
☐	WHITE FANG	Jack London	£1.25
☐	JESS AND THE RIVER KIDS	Judith O'Neill	£1.50
☐	A PATTERN OF ROSES	K. M. Peyton	£1.25
☐	YOU TWO	Jean Ure	£1.50
☐	SNOWY RIVER BRUMBY	Elyne Mitchell	£1.25

If you would like to hear more about Beaver Books, and discover all the latest news, don't forget the BEAVER BULLETIN. If you just send a stamped self-addressed envelope to Beaver Books, Brookmount House, 62-65 Chandos Place, Covent Garden, London WC2N 4NW, we will send you the latest BULLETIN.

If you would like to order books, please send this form, and the money due to:

HAMLYN PAPERBACK CASH SALES, PO BOX 11, FALMOUTH, CORNWALL, TR10 9EN.

Send a cheque or postal order, and don't forget to include postage at the following rates: UK: 55p for first book, 22p for second, 14p thereafter; BFPO and Eire: 55p for first book, 22p for second, 14p per copy for next 7 books, 8p per book thereafter; Overseas: £1.00 for first book, 25p thereafter.

NAME ....

ADDRESS ....

....

Please print clearly